URBAN CORRIDORS

Fables and Gables

Paul Levinson

TABLE OF CONTENTS

Prologue

Synchronicity
The Other Car
Extra Credit
The Wallet
The Last Train to Margaretville
Slipping Time
Ian, George, and George
Robinson Calculator

About the Author

Photograph on book cover by Emon Hassan
Published by Connected Editions, Inc.

To Tina, who inspired this all.

PROLOGUE

I suppose I'm better known for my science fiction than my fantasy, and it's my own fault. When I was younger, I even agreed with many science fiction writers that fantasy was "science fiction played with the net down". But lately, in the last decade or so, I've come around, as both a reader and a writer. So far, I've yet to write a fantasy novel, but my short fiction, published hither and yon, has increasingly been a kind of urban science fantasy. You'll find some of those stories below, along with the science fiction. They all take place, at least in part, in New York City. As far I know, none has anything resembling a net.

Enjoy!

-Paul Levinson, New York, August 2019

SYNCHRONICITY

First published in BuzzyMag, April 2014.

I t's been this way all of my life. Like when I was in high school, and we'd be reading our homework assignments out loud, and some kid would stand up right before me and read pretty much what I had written. Not that he'd cheated or anything. I never showed my work to anyone. And yet he'd written my ideas, even using my words. I had a hard time proving that *I* wasn't the cheat. "Great minds think alike," the more enlightened among my teachers would say. But that was too pat. I knew something else was going on — I just didn't know what.

It happened on the radio, too. I'd be singing a song, driving somewhere, and I turn on the radio and that very same song was playing. Yeah, I know that they played the Beatles a lot back then — still do on the oldies stations I listen to — but I mean, the Beatles have a pretty big catalog. What was the likelihood that "Dr. Robert" was on the radio right after I'd been singing it?

When I got to college and grad school, I began to search for similar patterns in history. There were plenty. Alexander Graham Bell and Elisha Gray invented the telephone, independently, at the same time. Pretty much the same for motion pictures — invented independently by Edison in the U.S., Friese-Greene in England, and the Lumière Bros in Paris. And of course Wallace came up with a theory of natural selection all on his own, at the same time as Darwin.

I was starting to put together a dissertation proposal on this very topic, when I came across an article published in an obscure journal — "On the Ubiquity of Independent, Simultaneous

Invention." I was crushed, but not really surprised. I left the doctoral program and took a job in my uncle's shoe store — I was in de feet, ha ha.

It was not that bad, though. I had no talent for shoe sales, so I wasn't vulnerable to the trauma of someone else coming up with my ideas. No danger of someone stealing my notion of a better display case, because I wouldn't have had that dumb idea in the first place. That was a relief. I went along like that for a good few years.

But the job also gave me lots of time to think and look around the Internet on my iPhone when there were no customers in the store. I began looking into quantum mechanics. Some scientists thought that just thinking about subatomic things was enough to affect them, and our mentalities might actually be in touch in some way with the past and the future, through some kind of time-unified quantum mechanical field. Maybe I and all the people who seemed to co-opt my ideas were connected to some future Omega point, the Platonic source of all ideas!

And sure enough, a few hours after I came up with that hypothesis, I found a book on Amazon on the exact same topic by some physicist I'd never heard of.

No problem. I should have known. Better to sell shoes. Yes, ma'am, we do have that style, and right in your size.

But the urge to break out of this is still strong, and I recently came up with another plan. Science fiction. Maybe if I presented what I know about this synchronicity not in a science book, but in a little science fiction story published somewhere online, it would slip under the radar. If it was not known in the future, maybe the quantum mechanical effect would keep it unknown to anyone but me until after it was published now, in the present. Lots of big ideas began with science fiction — Asimov and his robots, Verne and his submarines and rockets to the moon, right?

But I would have to be careful. Better not to think about this story too much, lest it make the synchronic leap. Better just write it and send it out.

(Sigh) And I just read what you are reading. The very same

story. My story. Hopeless case....

THE OTHER CAR

First published by Connected Editions, 2015.

I came down the stairs from the sports club and saw two identical cars. This surprised me, because only one of the cars was mine. I owned only a single car, no one else in the family had a car, and in fact I had driven here in that one car — a Prius hybrid I had bought about a year ago.

I looked more closely. Each of the two cars had the same license plate — mine — and they both had the same set of scuff marks on the rear left fender. One of the things I really liked about my Prius was how it unlocked automatically as I approached with its digital key in my pocket, but I couldn't always hear the unlocking, especially in an active, noisy parking lot like this one. I pulled open the door of the car which I was sure was mine — pretty sure, no, I was positive this was the space in which I had parked it about an hour ago, before my swim. There had been a big red Subaru next to it, on one side, and an empty space on the other.

The Subaru was still here, but now there was a Prius next to mine, identical to it from what I could see, in the space that had previously been empty. It had to be someone else's, even though it looked the same as mine, down to the plate, unless I was suffering from some kind of strange double vision. I guess someone could have been playing some kind of weird joke on me, someone who had the capacity to make up a phony license plate, and took the time to scout out my car and put similar scuffs on the rear fender. But who? And why?

I wondered if the chip in my keychain had opened this second car. I was tempted to see, but there were other people in the parking lot, and I didn't want the owner of this other car to see me breaking into it, if he or she came down the stairs or walked out of the elevator at the wrong time — but, on the other hand, who could blame me, the two cars seemed exactly the same.

I took a step towards the second car—

And she appeared, as if on cue. I'd noticed her and her bathing suit getting out of the pool. She gave me a slight smile now and opened the door to her Subaru. I pretended I had some business on my phone, and waited by my car until she left.

I looked again at the second car — still identical to mine — when my phone buzzed, now with some real business. Donna, the secretary in my Philosophy Department at Fordham University, was saying in a message that a student, Dava Hernandez, had an urgent problem regarding her mid-year graduation in February, which was just a month away, and could I come in to my office to see this student right away. "Dava would really appreciate it, Professor Oleson, thank you!" Going into the office was the last thing I wanted to do with this cloned car in my face, but I do like helping my students, and there was a book on my desk that I needed, so ... But I couldn't just leave that car.

I looked at the second Prius again, and continued debating with myself. I noticed a cop car had pulled up across the lot, likely to get a coffee at the Starbuck's, and that settled my debate. No way I was going to take a chance and break into a car that looked just like mine but couldn't be mine, with a cop just a few feet away. I waited a couple of minutes, anyway. But the officer looked like he was going to be on these premises for a while, sipping that hot latte or whatever it was.

I took a quick photo of the second car — I hope no one saw me — as I pulled away in mine. The license plate that was on this second Prius was indeed mine, and those scuffs were in the exact same place as on my car. I shook my head. I'd be back in this parking lot tomorrow — I went swimming every day — and could wait until then to see if there was anything more going on with this doppelganger car, or if it was a one-time inexplicable event. Hey, I could even drive back here after I saw the student.

***

I helped Dava with her problem, but struggled not to think about the second car as I was dispensing advice. I hoped what I was saying made sense — she seemed to think so — certainly what I was thinking made no sense to me.

I sighed after she left, grabbed the book I needed, and made to leave. I'd been gone from that parking lot by the pool just a little more than an hour. There was a chance that car which looked exactly like mine was still there, if I hadn't been imagining this whole experience in the first place. I checked the photograph I had taken — nope, I hadn't been imagining anything, unless I was imagining looking at this photograph. I proceeded down the stairs to my car. I patted it with affection — *this* was my car — and focused on what I might find by the pool.

I didn't get very far. The book I had just taken from my office — an old reprint edition of Albert Schwegler's *History of Philosophy* that I had picked up years ago — was also waiting for me in my car. Right next to me in the front seat. Not only the same edition, but with similar cracks on the olive-green cover and the same yellowing on the edges of the pages. I looked through the two books. Both had brown spots on pages 16, 27, and 52, in the exact same places. I stopped looking and closed my eyes. First the cars, now these books. I wrapped my hands around the books and squeezed hard. No, I wasn't imagining this.

What was going on? I had always thought it likely that my copy of Schwegler's book, translated by Julius Seelye, was the only copy now in existence — how many other copies of this 1888 translation of the German original, written years earlier, could there be? Libraries had probably discarded their copies more than half a century ago, and replaced them with more current histories of philosophy. I had purchased my copy for a dollar in a used book store near Bowdoin College in Maine in 2002, on a rare vacation trip. And now there were two copies in front of me, absolutely identical as far as I could see, down to the signature of the first owner, no doubt a student, one "Q. R. Smith, Bowdoin, '89," who had written that inscription in what was now faded brown ink — and was now in each of the books in front of me.

At least I had both books in my possession — unlike the cars — better proof than my photograph of the second car that this wasn't all in my mind. Even if I'd thought to photograph both cars side by side — which I wished I had — photographs were photoshopped and faked all the time. And anyone who looked at the photograph

I did have on my phone would no doubt say, right, it's a photograph of your car. I was the only who knew it was a photograph of a second car, identical to mine, right next to it in the parking lot.

But did I really know for sure that the second car, with or without the photograph, and these two books, were not just bizarre figments of my imagination? What had Samuel Johnson offered his biographer Boswell as proof that this world wasn't just God's dream? Kick that stone with my foot — if it hurts, the world is real. Except the pain could have been part of God's or Johnson's or anyone's dream, too — just as these twin books on my car seat, and the two cars in the parking lot, could be part of mine. True, all too true, except every ounce of my shaken being was screaming this wasn't a dream.

***

I slowly drove home — too upset now to go back to the sports club — with my hand on the two books, to make sure one didn't disappear. I needed to show the books to Jennifer, my wife, and tell her what was going on. Except I didn't know what was going on, certainly not the meaning of what I was seeing and now touching. But Jennifer had always been the more sensible of the two of us, her feet on the ground of medicine, a pediatrician, while my head was in the clouds of philosophy.

A crazed part of me wondered if I'd find that she, too, had split in two. Actually, that could be the least incredible of what I'd seen today — that Jennifer had a secret identical twin sister that she'd been keeping from me. I wondered if her twin would do exactly the same thing in bed ...

I was relieved to find that there was no car in our driveway, no identical twin of my Prius. Jennifer took a bus home from the medical center where she worked — it stopped about half a block from our house. I'd considered calling her and telling her about the cars and the books, but decided that this would be better done in person.

There were a pair of tulips in our garden — I hadn't noticed them before — but some kinds of tulips did that, didn't they, push up two flowers on one stem from a single bulb, right? Yeah, they were called multi-headed tulips, the way my own head was feeling right now.

Jennifer wasn't home, not even a single version of her. My phone buzzed with email — a message from Jennifer. It was a single message, but it said she was stuck with a patient having twins. This was quickly becoming a bad joke, except the punchline was on me, because I was staring at two books on the kitchen table now — the ones I had brought in from the car — the two exact same copies of Schwegler's *History of Philosophy*, down to the tear on the bottom right edge of page 61 in both books.

I had always found philosophy to be catnip for my mind — I could easily lose myself in Seelye's translation of Schwegler a thousandth time, read his cogent explanations of Kant that worked so well, and turn away from the world that seemed to be splitting in two around me. Cars, books—

I heard a sound at the door. It was the mailman pushing some envelopes through my door slot. Nothing surprising there. And if I did receive two pieces of identical
mail, hey, that happened from time to time with mass mailings. I picked up my envelopes and looked through the window at the mailman.

No, not the mailman. The mail *men*. There were two of them, and they looked exactly the same.

***

I yanked open the door. "Hey—," I shouted out.

The twin mailmen turned around. "Is everything ok?" one of them responded. "I'm pretty sure I got it right this time, and didn't give you anyone else's mail." He smiled.

"No, the mail is fine," I said. "I didn't know you were a twin."

Both men gave me an odd look.

"I have twins in my family," I lied, to explain my interest in these guys being twins.

They both nodded. "He's a mail carrier, too," one of them said. "We both like the same things."

Right, not surprising that identical twins like the same things, I thought, but why had I seen nothing of this twin before now? I suppose that was not surprising, either — but it certainly was incredible that I'd seen these twin mailmen the very same day as my two identical cars and two identical books, neither of which had existed in duplicate before, I was sure.

I was tempted to ask these mailmen if they had been twins before this instant — but they would have just thought I was nuts. I did have an opportunity, unlike with the cars and the books, to talk to these guys and maybe get some inkling about what was going on here in my life.

But what could I say to them? They were starting to leave. "So, tell me the truth, do you switch off on each other's routes?" I tried to think back over the four years we'd lived here. I'd had conversations with at least one of these guys from time to time, and I couldn't recall any time he had not remembered something we'd discussed or joked about previously.

"Right, we do that all the time," one of them replied, with a laugh, and the two turned and walked on to the next house.

I wondered what my neighbors, Jack and Susan Palmieri, would think of this. Would they be surprised by the twin mail carriers? Had they had just a single mailman until now, just as I had, and was their world now splitting apart, too? Somehow, I thought not.

Unfortunately, neither Jack nor Susan seemed to be home. The mailmen delivered their mail and walked on.

But I noticed Jack and Susan's car was in their driveway — maybe one or both of them was inside their house, after all, and just hadn't come to the door. I might as well see if they were home, and talk to them if they were there.

***

Susan answered the door. She was dressed in jeans and a sweater and looked good. "James," she said and smiled at me, as she bent down to pick up her mail. Something about her form was familiar — yeah, her body reminded me of the woman in the bathing suit at the pool, the red Subaru driver. Why hadn't I noticed

this before? I put it out of my mind now — thinking about my neighbor's wife like this didn't make sense for all kinds of reasons.

"Uhm, this might sound like a stupid question," I began. I decided to ask her a question that was anything but stupid, and could be crucial to my understanding what was happening to me.

She looked up from her mail. "Sure — the kids ask me stupid questions all the time." She flashed a bright smile.

"Well, I don't know if you noticed the mailmen," I replied, "but did you know they were twins? With all the mail fraud going on these days, and identity thefts, you can't be too careful about who is delivering your mail."

She gave me a strange look.

That was indeed a stupid point, I thought to myself — what did twin mailmen have to do with identity theft? But the question was important — did my neighbor know that the mailman had a twin? If she did, then what I had just seen was maybe just a wild coincidence, given the books and the cars. If not—

She shook her head no. "News to me," she said, and walked out on to her driveway, and looked down the street. The twin mailmen were nowhere to be seen.

"Mommy!" her eight year-old daughter, Samantha, called out from inside. "Daniel took my cupcake!"

"I did not!" Daniel protested.

Susan gave me an apologetic look, and walked back into her house. Yeah, she definitely looked like the woman from the pool, from behind, too.

***

I walked back into my house, and hit the laptop — I still preferred that to my phone when seeking maximum information.

A few minutes of searching brought up Wernicke-Korsakoff

syndrome — but, other than the double vision, that syndrome had little in common with what I'd been experiencing. I had no loss of memory — as far as I knew — and no loss of muscle coordination, either. I looked in the mirror — my eyelids weren't drooping. I wasn't an alcoholic — I had maybe a glass or two of red wine a month. I had no vitamin B1 deficiency that I knew of — one of the causes of this syndrome — I took a multi-vitamin every day, and it had plenty of B1. I took the vitamin bottle out of the kitchen cabinet and checked — yep, 1.5 milligrams of vitamin B1 in every pill, 100% of daily requirements, the label said. I was certain that I'd taken one of these pills after breakfast this morning, but I popped another in my mouth now just to be sure.

I thought again about memory loss. I guess that would explain why I'd seen the twin mailmen, with no recollection of seeing them before, if they had indeed come by only once in a while. If that's what had happened, Susan's not seeing them could just be the result of her not being home the few times the twins had made their deliveries.

But I looked again at the two copies of Schwegler. Unless I was flat out psychotic and hallucinating, the two identical copies were clearly in front of me now. Hallucinations were unfortunately one of the symptoms of Korsakoff syndrome, but how could I prove these two identical books were or were not an hallucination? Go back to Susan and ask if she saw one or two copies of Schwegler? If she hadn't thought I was out of my mind about the mailmen, asking her about the two books
would definitely seal it. And whatever she said, that could be part of my hallucination, too. There was no escaping the tentacles of the Johnson-Boswell infinite regress when it came to this.

I shook my head and tried another tack. I looked up real, undeniable examples of doubling. They were everywhere — binary fission of bacteria and single-celled organisms happened all the time. And bilateral symmetry in higher-level organisms was every place you looked — we humans had two arms, two legs, two eyes, two ears, two cheeks, two breasts, and lots of other parts of our bodies that came in pairs. Those twosomes all started out the same in the fetus, before the wear and tear of living took its toll and made one arm a little different from the other, one ear lobe pierced, and gave each member of the pair its own identity.

So what was I? Someone experiencing double vision illusions or a true binary division of the world into some kind of alternate? If I was indeed at the center of a world undergoing binary fission, that would be a new wrinkle in the Gaia hypothesis that the world was a single, unified organism. Was I some kind of witness to a bilateral symmetry beginning to emerge in the reality around me?

One thing I was sure of: if that was what was happening, if reality itself was starting to split in two, if that's what the cars and the books and the mailmen were all about, I was an unwilling witness in the extreme. I had never volunteered for this. I wanted no part of the world's partition.

And if "this" — whatever exactly that was — was really happening — wasn't that crazier, sicker, far more insane, than any kind of psychosis or syndrome?

I shook my head again, to clear it of some of these desperately complex cobwebs, and only barely succeeded. I looked again at the two identically worn Schwegler books — they were my best proof, my only proof in hand, that I wasn't hallucinating. I picked up the two books. Or, if I was hallucinating, this was far more than a visual hallucination — something far more profound than an optical illusion, psychotic or otherwise.

I put the books down and exhaled. I needed more evidence. I looked at the clock on my kitchen wall. It was only about two hours since I'd been at the pool, even though it felt like a lifetime ago. But there was still a chance that the other car which looked just like mine, down to the license plate and the scrapes on the fender, was still there.

***

It was 12-minute drive from my home to the sports club, exactly 12 minutes, I'd timed it many times. I took the two copies of Schwegler with me, I didn't want to let them out of my sight and grasp. I thought over my situation, this impossible situation, as I drove. Was I really at the center, the nucleus, of reality splitting in two? Egotistical, I know, but I preferred that to being insane. And if reality was indeed undergoing some kind of binary split, and it was for some reason starting with me, or what was happening around me, what would happen when the split was complete, when the fission had yielded two realities where previously there had been but one? Would there be two versions of me — two "me"s, one in each reality? And would we start out exactly the same, perfect duplicates, but gradually go our slightly separate ways, maybe like two legs, one of which had a scar and the other not?

I pulled into the sports club parking lot. A Japanese gentleman — whom I'd seen many times in the pool — was opening the door of his car. Thank goodness he had no twin — or, if he had, the twin wasn't with him now. I drove carefully around the lot, very carefully, but there was no other car there like mine, not even another Prius. I was waiting for the other car to drop, an irreverent part of my brain piped up. I told it to shut up. Then I began to rejoice — there was no other Prius! None like mine or anyone else's in the parking lot! Maybe the vitamin B was working! Then I looked at the two copies of Schwegler's book on my seat. No, this aspect of the binary fission, at least, was still very much in evidence, down to the Q. R. Smith on two pages in two books in faded brown ink.

I always kept an extra bathing suit in my car. Why not go upstairs to the pool for a swim? It would clear my head — I did some of my best thinking with it briefly underwater. I did ten laps, breast stroke. I'd left the books on a towel on a lounge chair by the pool, so I could see them when I was swimming. I climbed out of the pool, dried off, and took the books to my locker. I dressed quickly.

Two men were having a conversation about going to the Daily Double at Yonkers Raceway tonight, which caught my attention.

"I was going to bet on Enchanted Pair. But the temperature's supposed to drop like a stone," one of the men said. "Will it be too cold for the horses to run?"

The other man laughed. "The horse is a North American

animal — they don't give a damn about the cold."

I was tempted to point out that horses actually came from the steppes of Asia, but no one had asked for my opinion. Then I thought, hey, for all I know, maybe I'm in an alternate reality already, and in this reality horses originated in North America. Great. The swim had been relaxing, but had made me no less insane, if that's what I was.

I walked quickly down the stairs to my car. There was just one car. I drove around the parking lot again, very slowly. Still no other cars exactly like mine, no other Priuses at all. I began to drive home. Maybe whatever had been happening — to me, to reality, to both — was subsiding. But I still had the twin books on the car seat.

***

I passed by the Jelly Fish, a summer sports store on the corner, closed now, and that got me thinking. What did an amoeba feel when it split in half? It was a blob of jelly, and it had no feelings, not even any perceptions, the way higher animals did. All that an amoeba knew of its world is what it bumped into at any instant. But if the amoeba had a mind, what would it be thinking when it split in half? Would it suddenly have two separate trains of thought, both going back to a common source, the amoeba before it split?

What would I experience, would I be thinking, if I somehow split in half — if the cars, the books, the two mailmen were the beginning of a mitosis I was already undergoing? Would I end up with two streams of perceptions and thoughts at the same time? No, that would be crazy. Really crazy. Crazier by a greater order of magnitude than what I'd been going through today. I patted the two Schweglers on the seat and laughed ruefully to myself. Crazy? I was already there with these books and everything that had been happening these past few hours. I needed to
speak to Jennifer. She was a doctor — she'd know what to do. I tried her again on the phone and got voicemail. She was likely still tied up with those twins — real twins, a sarcastic part of my brain said, in my mother's voice.

I pulled into my empty driveway. No mailmen were in sight. The two tulips were still in the garden, but they were by far the least extraordinary of the pairs I'd been encountering.

I took the books with me, and went upstairs to shower. Yeah, a nice long shower, to wash off the chlorine and soothe my mind some more. Showers, like swimming, were always conducive to some of my best thinking. I put the two Schweglers on the bed, and stroked them, almost protectively. I'd always loved the book, but this was something more. The two identical volumes, with the same exact flecks on the spines, were somehow sweet proof that maybe I wasn't crazy. No, nothing was sweet about this. But these two books were my touchstones of reality, such as it now was for me.

***

The hot shower felt good, just as I'd expected. There was something not only cleansing but generative about water. It was after all the place in which in we, all individuals and I guess all life, were born. Now, as the water and the steam enveloped me, I wondered if some other rendition of me was also taking a shower, also enjoying the hot water right now. I suppose there could be an infinite number of "me"s right now, but would we each be taking a shower or doing different things? The key was not really the number, and what each of us may have been doing, but what knowledge we might have of these other, alternate lives. As Schwegler explained so clearly, Kant had said that there were aspects of existence, maybe the deepest aspects, that were so far from our perception that we could never really know them at all — the "thing-in-itself," was the usual translation, meaning, the object, the reality, that existed underneath whatever perception we may have had of it. But, as Ernst Haeckel had remarked about a hundred years after Kant, if some deep aspect of reality existed that we could never have any knowledge of at all, what did it matter, why even bother to think and talk about it?

I vigorously shook my head no — this bifurcation, this binary fission that I seemed to be experiencing in some way, was something I was very much aware of. That was precisely the problem—

My phone was ringing. Could be Jennifer. I stepped out of the shower, grabbed a towel, and went for the phone, which I had left on the bathroom sink.

"Honey," it was Jennifer, "had a hell of a day, but I'm just about finished here. I see you called?"

"Yeah," I said. "How about dinner at Taverna?" I knew I didn't want to tell her about my worse than hellish day on the phone – difficult conversations always went down better over dinner.

"Sounds wonderful, I'm famished," Jennifer said. "Those twins took a long time coming out, but all's well that ends well."

"I'm glad," I said. "I love you."

"Me too," Jennifer said. "I should be home in about 45 minutes."

"Great — see you then," I said.

***

I finished toweling, and put on some fresh clothes. That shower and Jennifer's call had done me a lot of good. I felt better than I had felt since I'd first seen that other car, exactly like mine, at the sports club. That felt like a long time ago, now.

I put on my pairs of socks and shoes. They were identical twins, too, but unlike the books, had been that way from the get-go. I looked at my bed. I hadn't thought about the two identical Schwegler books since I'd walked into the shower. I'd left the two copies on the bed. There was just one book there now.

***

I didn't know whether to laugh or cry. This meant, what, that my world was not actually splitting in two and that I had indeed been suffering some kind of profound hallucination that included holding two books in my hand, when there really had been only one? And this insane illusion had ended now, why, because the extra vitamin I had taken had finally been absorbed by my system and had its recuperative effect?

I looked around the room, under the bed, frantic to find the second book — no, this was not a time to be frantic but happy, relieved, that this psychotic double vision had apparently ended.

I looked under the bed a second time. Nothing there but dust and a stray piece of paper or two. I should be jumping up and down with joy about this — yes, this was good. That had to be right. I'd had a mental episode of some unfathomable kind, gone postal with the mailmen and the books and the cars for a couple of hours, but that had been corrected by the vitamin B. I'd talk to Jennifer about all of this over dinner — maybe all I needed was some vitamin therapy.

I took the single copy of Schwegler in my hand, and walked slowly downstairs. There were tears in my eyes now. What a day, what a day. Is this the way it started for people who lost their minds? I didn't know. I still didn't feel that I'd lost my mind, at all, today. Was that all part of the syndrome?

It had all begun with that other car, identical down to the scrapes in the paint job to mine. I put on a coat — it was beginning to get really cold outside — and gave my car a close examination. It was the only car in my driveway, that was good. And it seemed no different from the way it had been, none the worse for it apparently having been the victim of a clone. No, a clone of my mind's own making, if all that I had been suffering today was not the birth of a second reality but just a shredding of my perception.

I breathed in deeply and looked around. No double mailmen on the street, either. I guessed that if I waited here until tomorrow's mail delivery, all I'd see was one mailman. My neighbor Susan must have thought I was having some kind of mental lapse — I hope I hadn't overly disconcerted her with my questions.

I looked up and down the street and turned back to the house. Wait— what about the photograph of the second Prius I had taken at the sports club? I'd forgotten about that — would it be gone too? I reached into my pocket for my phone—

But I saw something on the street in the periphery of my vision. It was a car coming around the corner. Damn, it was a Prius, just like mine.

Okay, okay, there were lots of Prius's in Westchester. I stood on my doorstep and watched the approaching car.

It was indeed just like mine. I tried not to look at the driver, or if there were any passengers. But I couldn't turn away. Would this car pull into my driveway, right next to mine?

My eyes were on the driver. But I saw Jennifer sitting next to him. Had someone with a Prius, another doctor, given her a ride home?

No, that wasn't it. I looked at the driver. He looked at me. Our eyes locked for a minute. I needed a photo of this. I shoved the phone in front of my face and snapped. There was a huge bright flash, even though it was broad daylight—

And I drove on, with Jennifer clutching my hand.

EXTRA CREDIT

First published in Buzzy Mag, *July 2012.*

Jon 1

Jon slammed the piece of mail on the table, knocking off a buttered half of bagel in the process. It teetered on its edge on the floor for a moment, then fell down squarely on the buttered side.

"Another wrong credit card charge," he called up to Trudi between curses. "Seems we stayed at the Coach and Chariot Inn last month."

"With or without the kids?" Trudi walked in and sighed. She picked up the credit card statement and shook her head. "This is — what? — the third mistake like this since the new year?"

"Cancel the card." Jon scooped up the bagel, surveyed the sticky dust, and tossed the bagel in the garbage. "If these people are too lame to get their charges straight, we'll go elsewhere."

"We need the credit line," Trudi said. "I just got a cash advance —"

"Do whatever you want, then." Jon waved his hand in disgust. "But let's at least call the company and explain that we were at your mother's house getting heartburn on her cooked-to-death chicken when they say we were in the whirlpool at the Chariot."

"Right," Trudi said, "as soon as I finish with the Motor Vehicles people about why my new registration isn't here yet. And my mother's chicken is manna from heaven compared to your mother's hydrochloric pot roast."

***

The woman on the speaker-phone was about what Jon and Trudi expected. "Have you folks moved recently?" she asked.

"No, we've been here for four years," Trudi said.

"Has your mail been reported stolen recently? That's the start of a lot of identity theft."

"Uh, no," Trudi said. There was that time several months ago when their mail had been mixed in with several of their neighbors' little bundles of mail, but nothing had wound up lost as far as she knew. It was pretty funny, though, seeing the kind of pornography that old Mr. Gleason up the street subscribed to.

"And you're certain you and your husband didn't sneak away for a quickie at the Chariot—"

"Believe me, we're certain," Jon replied.

"Well, I don't know what to tell you then," the woman said earnestly. "The hotel admits that they have no physical record of your being there — no signed receipts, or that sort of thing. But their computer record is quite clear that you were there."

"Haven't you people ever heard of computer hackers?" Jon asked. Jeez.

"Well of course we have, Mr. Goldman. But what would a hacker stand to gain by charging a room to your credit card, and not using the room?"

"I don't know," Jon said. "Look, I'm not Sherlock Holmes — I can't tell what makes a criminal tick. I just want this charge taken off my credit card."

"Well, of course. I already told you that the hotel has no physical evidence of your having been there, so of course we'll remove the charge. But we'd like to get to the bottom of this."

"So would we," Trudi said. "What do you propose?"

"Well, for a start, we're putting a special photo-hold on your card. Starting today, you and your husband won't be able to use your card without showing a photo-ID to the retailer. And of course no mail orders or phone or computer orders will be allowed."

"Fine," Trudi said, sarcastically. "We're the ones getting hacked, but we're the ones being treated now like criminals. Fine."

"We're doing this for your benefit, Mrs. Goldman."

"For your benefit, too — these credit thefts cost you time and money," Jon said.

"Which all comes back to you, Mr. Goldman, because these losses oblige us to raise the interest you and our other card holders pay us. Anything more I can help you with today?"

***

Jon rifled through the Saturday morning mail. "Card from Auntie Kira in Florida ...
bill from the plumber ... something from Chandler at MIT, I don't know why he didn't send this to me at the lab—"

"Any mail for me, Dad?"

Jon smiled at his eight-year old son. "Yep, here's a card from Ari. Looks like it has something scribbled on the back."

Noah laughed. "It's a code, Dad."

"Ah. And here's something for you, sweetheart." Jon handed a piece of colorful advertising over to Samantha, their two-year old, who promptly put it in her mouth.

"No, no, that's not good for you honey." Trudi leaned over and pulled the advertisement away. "That's good to look at, not—"

"Goddamn charge again!" Jon exploded. He waved the statement in the air. "This one's nineteen dollars and twenty-eight cents — from the Parthenon diner three weeks ago. We didn't eat there then, did we?"

"No, and we wouldn't have gotten out of that goldmine for so little if we had." Trudi took the statement and stared. She pulled her phone out of her pocket and jabbed a number.

"Look, I know it's a Saturday," she said tersely into the phone after giving her credit card number, "but I want to speak to your supervisor. Right. It's about the fourth wrong charge to our credit card this year, this time from a diner that we last ate in maybe six months ago. That's right, we have a photo-hold on our card and everything. Thank you."

"We should sue them, Mom," Noah said. "I hate that place—"

"Shhh!" Jon held up a warning finger. Meanwhile, Samantha deftly pushed her father's plate so that it was just about half over the edge of the table, where it sat with the half-eaten scrambled eggs interrupted by the morning mail delivery.

"That's right," Trudi was talking again. "It's getting to the point where this card is more trouble than it's worth — my husband and I have to look at every statement like hawks to make sure we're not being charged for something that— Right. I know there's a lot of this kind of theft going on and you're doing your best to control it. But—"

Trudi took the phone away from her ear in exasperation and held it out at arm's length. The supervisor's voice was squeaking about people needing to be careful about crooks looking over their shoulders in department stores when charging merchandise. Then he said something about a new retinal scan that the credit card company was introducing—

"Cancel the card already," Jon said. "I've had it with this!" He jabbed in the air to make his point. His elbow brushed his plate — and pushed it over the edge. It landed face down on the floor with his eggs. There was something going on here that, given half a chance, was definitely working against him.

Jon 2

A slightly different universe, almost the same as ours in all respects...

Jon kissed Trudi full on the lips at the front door. "So we're finally making a little progress on the finances," he said.

"We're still in debt," Trudi said.

"I know, but at least we're starting to move now in the right direction." He blew Trudi another kiss and walked to his Prius in the driveway. The doors clicked open at his approach. This Prius was one of the reasons they were in debt so deeply. Jon knew this, but also felt that the Prius was worth every penny.

The drive from home to Fordham University was precisely 18 minutes. This was one of the things Jon loved about his job. He parked his car, walked quickly to Everett Hall, and bounded up the three flights of stairs to the Theoretical Physics Digital Lab. He grabbed a cup of coffee from the shiny new machine and entered his little sanctum.

Eugene, the current grad assistant, was already hard at work, rendering some old analog video clips into digital. Jon clapped him on the back and proceeded to his own workstation. There was a piece of mail on the desk. Jon shook his head.

"Mailroom brought it up just a few minutes ago," Eugene offered. "Another missive from Scott Chandler — you going to just throw it out like the others?"

Jon played with the envelope and laughed. "You know, it's sad. He says he sends his really important messages through land mail, because he's afraid his email doesn't always get read. And now I'm proving that the same can happen to paper mail." Jon tossed the envelope. It made a neat fluttering descent into the trash basket.

Eugene chuckled. "It's the price of your success. You attract crackpots."

Jon started up his desktop. No one other than Jon — not even Eugene — knew what Jon had here. Jon scarcely believed it himself. His Russian former graduate assistant, apparently a budding computer genius, had left it in this machine. "My gift to you," she had told him, "to thank you for being such an inspiring teacher."

Jon called up the program, started work on a transaction—

"Jon." Jill Barnes, a colleague, was in the doorway. "We're due at that faculty meeting in 15 minutes."

"Right." Jon cursed to himself, and logged off the machine. He'd forgotten about the stupid meeting, which he was obliged to attend. He shut off his computer, and smiled at Jill. "Let's go then."

He took his coffee and waved goodbye to Eugene as he left the office. Eugene thought about it for a few minutes after Jon was gone, then quickly fished Chandler's letter out of Jon's trash.

Jon 1

Our universe...

Jon entered the digital lab, sipping a cup of perfectly brewed coffee. He wrestled his suddenly ringing phone out of his pocket, narrowly missing the coffee as he put the phone to his ear and mouth. "Yah, good, honey," he said to Trudi. "We'll do fine with just the bank card. We did the right thing canceling the Ameri—" He realized he was talking loudly, and Eugene could hear. "Ok, good," he said quietly to Trudi. He put the phone away, nodded to Eugene and sat at his temporary computer station.

It had been temporary for almost two months now, and he felt bad about that, not only because he had been deprived of his own work place, but because his old desk had had Sasha's present upon it. She had given it to him as a parting gift, before she'd decamped for her doctorate at Cal Tech. "Something very special for your computer," she had told him. "My gift to you, to thank you for all the extra credit and belief you have given me."

Not quite the perfect construction, but that was Sasha, better at code than words. He looked at the computer now on his temporary desk, his current computer, and sighed. Some student had spilled soda on his computer with Sasha's present the day after Sasha had left. Hey, if faculty didn't follow the no food and drink in the lab rules, why should the students? And he had never had a chance to even touch his original computer since then. It had been out for repair, the techies still not clear exactly what was wrong with it—

"Jon." That would be Jill Barnes, here to walk with him to a faculty meeting as per their appointment. "We're due at the meeting in 15 minutes." He'd have rather walked himself, but what could he do, he couldn't be rude to a colleague.

"Right." He stood and knocked over his coffee. He'd barely had a sip. He cursed to himself, but smiled at Jill.

"I'll clean it up, you'll be late," Eugene said.

"Oh, thanks!" Jon said. He turned to Jill. "Let's go then."

"Some mail came in for you," Eugene called out as Jon joined Jill at the doorway. "I'll get it when I come back," Jon said.

Jon 2

The slightly different universe...

"What do you think they'll tell us about the salary freeze?" Jill asked Jon, as they walked across the campus.

Jon winced slightly in the sharp February breeze. "Won't make much difference to me, one way or the other, given my mortgage." And also the fact that he'd tapped into the new source of income.

"Yeah, tell me about it," Jill said, referring to the high cost of living. Jon nodded. He didn't like talking about this.

"I just think it's wrong that they increase the number of students in our classes, but keep our salaries on hold," Jill continued. "I mean, I know the economy's still uneven, but enrollment has been up and—"

Jon's ringing phone interrupted Jill's critique. Jon was grateful. He smiled apologetically at Jill, threw his nearly empty coffee cup into a nearby receptacle and took the call. "Hey, on my way to a meeting," he said to Trudi.

"Oh, right, sorry," Trudi said. "The meeting about the salary freeze?"

"Yeah," Jon replied.

"Well, don't let them intimidate you. You're entitled—"

"I know."

"Ok. I just had a quick question — about a new after-school possibility for Noah. Can you talk?"

"Sure. More or less," Jon replied.

"Well, the school has some wild-bird expert who'll be running a special program in identifying migrant birds in the New York area. You know how much Noah loves that."

Jon nodded. "Absolutely."

"But it'll cost us $200," Trudi said. "I know we've been doing better with that long-range installment plan you worked out for us online, but—"

"Let's do it." They'd been doing a *lot* better with that "installment" plan, which required no payment at all, not even for the purchases themselves.

"Ok," Trudy said, mostly happily, but with a tinge of unassuaged concern.

"We're here," Jon told Trudi, as he and Jill reached their

destination. Jill scowled, in continuing anger at the university administration.

Jon 1

Our universe...

The walk across campus was uneventful. Jill was droning on about the outrage of the salary freeze, but Jon had more pressing financial problems to think about. What the hell was going on with his credit card? Ok, he'd canceled the one with the phantom charges, but why couldn't the credit card company get to the bottom of it? And if he was being targeted by some super hacker who had acquired his credit card, what was to stop him or her from moving to another one of Jon's cards?

His phone rang. It was likely Trudi. Jon didn't answer. He needed to think about this more. But he didn't blame his wife in the slightest for being so worried. He supposed the next step would be to go to the police, but Jon didn't relish being an official victim of anything, and the time that would take out of life.

He and Jill reached the meeting hall. Her talk subsided into a scowl about the university administration.

Faculty were milling around the hall, breath visible and frosty this early February afternoon. Jon looked them over. The usual suspects talking about their same First World problems ... Oleson and Klein to the left of him, Hentoff and Cleary to the right, the President of the Faculty Senate and her entourage in the middle. He was not particularly close to any of them — he often said he preferred his students to his colleagues — and—

Wait a minute! Jeez! Was that Chandler? Yes, it was, and he was walking right towards Jon, and it was too late for Jon to pretend he didn't see him.

"Jonathan!" Chandler extended a big, beefy hand.

"Scott — good to see you — what brings you to the Bronx?"

"I was visiting Liu in the Math Department — we're doing a conference together next year — and I called your office, and your grad assistant told me you were on your way here. I've been trying to talk to you about something for a few weeks now. I'm not completely sure what it means, but—"

"Why didn't you call or email?" Jon knew the answer, but saw no advantage in making this easier for Chandler.

"I don't like talking about these things on the phone," Chandler said in a conspiratorial tone. "Same thing with email. I was only calling your office to see if you were in, so I could drop by. I did send you a few letters, by the way — in fact, I sent one just last week, letting you know I'd be on campus today."

Jon shook his head derisively. "Mail is getting less reliable every day."

Jill, who had joined the Hentoff-Cleary conversation, waved at Jon. "I'm going in," she mouthed at Jon in exaggerated motions and walked to the entrance way.

Jon was glad for the excuse to get to the point with Chandler, who had seen Jill's departure. "Ok, so what did you want to talk to me about?" he asked Chandler. "I'm sure it will be more stimulating than what I'll hear in there." He gestured to the building. He realized that that was likely, sadly true.

"I ran into a student of yours in California last month," Chandler's tone was lower and more conspiratorial, "Sasha Humek?"

Jon nodded.

"And, well, I guess she had too much vodka," Chandler continued. "She's brilliant, you know. Her paper on inter-alter-matrices was really something — raised a lot of eyebrows. All hypothetical, of course."

"Yes," Jon replied.

"But she had had a lot to drink, as I told you," Chandler said, "and I couldn't completely understand her — you know, between the accent and the drink."

Jon nodded again.

"But I think she said something about actually developing a program that could do that," Chandler said, "and I've been thinking about that ever since, and it's been bothering me."

"Do what?" Jon asked.

Jon 2

The slightly different universe...

Jon looked around at the faculty walking and talking around the front of the building, like geese honking on a lawn. Jeez — there was that noodge Chandler! What the hell was he doing here, stalking Jon? Jon spun around quickly, neatly, and walked away, to the other side of the building. He thought he heard Jill telling him she was going in. He waved over his shoulder without turning around. He didn't want to risk Chandler spotting him, if he hadn't already.

Jon thought he knew what Chandler wanted to talk to him about — he had read Chandler's first letter. Jon had thought then that it would be best to avoid this conversation for as long as he possibly could. He had the same opinion now.

Jon ducked into a side door, then into a men's room, and hoped this would be the last he would see of Scott Chandler. Oleson from Philosophy was drying in his hands in the super blade or whatever it was called new dryer. He nodded at Jon and left.

Jon figured he'd hang out in the bathroom until the meeting got underway, walk carefully to the rear entrance, and look around. He doubted Chandler would wait around if he didn't see Jon either entering the meeting or in the meeting once it had started. Then Jon realized that the safest course of action, if he wanted to avoid Chandler, was to leave this hall altogether, and just go home without attending the meeting at all. Jon knew he could count on Jill to attest that he had indeed been here, even if she didn't see him leave after the meeting. What kind of psycho, after all, would walk all the way across campus to a meeting, only to walk out before it started?

As for Chandler, he'd survive. True, Chandler had sent Trudi and him congratulations cards when Noah and Samantha were born, but that wasn't the important thing now. Jon had to protect his kids from the financial vicissitudes that sooner or later struck everyone, especially in the current world.

Jon 1

Our universe...

Two late-arriving faculty walked quickly by Jon and Chandler — Chandler pulled back from Jon and held a finger to his lips. "We shouldn't just be standing here, talking in the open like this," he said, in a volume so low now that Jon could barely hear.

Jon looked at the hall in which the meeting was about to commence, and thought quickly: No one will miss me at this point if I don't attend this. Jill would say to anyone who asked that she had walked with me to the meeting, and who would be so crazy as to walk all the way to a faculty meeting, only to walk away before the meeting started? Well, maybe not so crazy, for anyone who knew how boring faculty meetings could be, but—

Jon realized that Chandler was waiting for a response, and beginning to edge even further away. "Of course," Jon answered. "You're right, of course. Let's just take a nice little stroll around the campus — we'll be able to see anyone we're approaching, or approaching us, and we can stop talking if need be." Jon took Chandler's arm, and began escorting him away from the building.

Chandler nodded slowly, reluctantly. "But your meeting?"

"It's ok," Jon replied. "My colleagues will fill me in. So, you were about to tell me what Sasha told you, in her Russian accent, when she was a little drunk."

"A lot drunk," Chandler said.

Jon nodded.

"And she—" Chandler started and stopped talking in deference to two students who were walking by.

"Hi Professor!" one of them said brightly to Jon.

"Hey, Dava, how are you doing?" Jon replied. Then, to Chandler, "And?"

"And your student Sasha told me she had written a program that permitted inter-alternate-universal transactions."

"Come again?"

"Don't play dumb with me," Chandler replied, suddenly losing all of his trepidation. "You know exactly what I mean — she was your student. If she really wrote such a program she must have learned it from you."

Jon considered. "She was one of those students who already knew a lot more than I did the first day she stepped into my class, that's why she was my grad assistant," he said, truthfully. "Did she tell you what she intended to do with such a program?"

"She said she was leaving it and the decision about whether and how to use it in your hands."

Jon said nothing. He knew where the program likely was, now. "You going to pretend you know nothing of this?" Chandler pushed.

"Some student spilled sticky soda on my computer before I even had a chance to load Sasha's program."

"So you've never used Sasha's program?" Chandler asked, not completely believing what Jon had just told him.

"No," Jon replied, and his eyes flared with the beginning of understanding. "But that does not mean it has not been used."

Jon 2

The slightly different universe...

Jon was in his Prius, ignition on, when he realized he had left the transaction he had started in his office incomplete — interrupted by Jill and their apparent need to go to that stupid meeting. But the meeting was no longer an issue. So what was keeping him from his desk and that transaction?

Chandler could come looking for him in the office, after not being able to locate Jon at the meeting, but Jon had no intention living the rest of his life in fear of a conversation with Chandler. And completing the transaction in the office shouldn't take more than a minute.

Jon grinned as he turned the car off, stepped out, locked it, left it, and made his way back to his office. The nice thing about being so way beyond the cutting edge was no one could see what you were doing, even if you were doing it right before their very eyes.

Well, he supposed one person could. Not a person in this universe, this reality, though. But the Jon in that other universe, the Jon whose card was being charged for his, this Jon's, purchases: he would certainly see the results, he of course would see the charges and would feel their impact.

But a few charges certainly couldn't bankrupt anybody. They might cause a little discomfort, a little concern, but, hey, for all Jon knew, his alternate self was a rich man, a millionaire, who wouldn't feel or mind the little debits at all. Hey, Jon had come close to making it big in this world himself — a better book deal, more high-paying jobs as a consultant to complement his teaching career, any one of a dozen slightly different breaks could have put him in the upper strata right now. For all Jon knew, his alternate self had done all of this and more, and wouldn't notice or care at all about a charge from a hotel he had never slept in.

Jon bounded up the three flights of stairs to his office.

Jon 1

Our universe...

Jon was determined to get a look at Sasha's program and get to the bottom of this insanity. Could the inexplicable charges on his credit card really be the result of some alter-self of his, in an alternate, parallel universe, having made the charges, but via Sasha's program somehow transferred those charges to Jon's credit card right here in Jon's universe? Jon fingered the card in his wallet inside his jacket pocket, then clenched and unclenched his fist in anger. "I think I know where my computer with the program is right now," he said to Chandler. "You want to come with me to our tech repair center?"

It couldn't hurt to have Chandler standing by, in case Jon had trouble using the program — assuming his beleaguered computer was in some sort of working condition now. Jon was good with computers, but Chandler was better, a classic nerd case of clumsy with people, smooth with equipment. Conceivably he could get Jon's computer to work, when Jon and the techies could not.

"Sure," Chandler replied. "Locate the program and destroy it — leaving it out there in the world is not a good idea."

"Exactly," Jon lied, as the two approached the gleaming new IT center. He had no intention of destroying Sasha's little present to him — at least, not before he'd had a chance to use it, and set the universes straight. And maybe make a little profit for himself. He thought for a second about disinviting Chandler— no, unless Jon's computer was resurrected, he would not be able to even get a look at Sasha's program.

Jon 2

The slightly different universe...

Jon sat at his work station. Eugene was nowhere to be seen — he was probably out to lunch. Good. Although Jon didn't worry much about doing his special transactions with Eugene around — who would not have known what he was looking at, if he'd happened to have glanced at Jon's screen — Jon still preferred doing this with no possibly prying eyes over his shoulder.

Jon booted up his computer. He went directly into that miraculous little program Sasha had provided. He clicked the icon that would make it work now in the background, as Jon went to the Fieldstone school web site — Fieldstone was Noah's school — and made the $200 payment for Noah's afterschool bird-identification course. And the sweet, incredible thing was that this charge would never show up on his credit card. Sasha's program would shunt it to the parallel universe, where it would be charged to Jon's alternate self's card.

He finished the transaction, and leaned back in his chair, with his hands clasped around the back of his neck. Ethical issues aside, this was indeed one fine piece of business. It thrilled him as much as it had the first time he had attempted it. Trans-universe transactions were positively addicting.

Jon 1

Our universe...

Jon walked into the head-tech's office, with Chandler a little behind him. "Professor Jon Goldman," Jon announced to the head-tech, and pulled out his faculty ID.

"I know who you are," the head-tech said, without a trace of a smile.

"Good. Well, I'd-"

"You'd like your computer back and working. I know. Your office has called here, what, a dozen times?"

"The computer's been out of commission for nearly two months — all because a little soda was spilled on it?" Jon had long ago realized there was no point matching attitudes with these IT people. They held his equipment in their hands — they held all the cards. Still, it was hard to resist the bait.

"As I know I already told you, it's something more than the ginger ale," the techie explained, his patience already strained. "We replaced the damaged parts, but we can't get it to keep working for more than a few minutes once we turn it on. We think it's some kind of virus that got in there before the liquid, and it's incompatible with the upgrade hardware we put in. We're still trying to identify it. We have an obligation to make sure it doesn't spread to other computers on the campus."

Chandler spoke up. "Can we — Professor Goldman — see the machine? If that's possible."

The head-tech shrugged. "Won't do you much good."

"I know," Chandler said, soothingly, "but—"

The techie shrugged and pointed to the other room. "It's against the far wall in there."

Jon and Chandler proceeded to the room. "Glad I brought you along," Jon told Chandler. "You have a good way with these people."

Chandler just nodded. Jon looked at the far wall. "Ah! There it is."

He and Chandler proceeded to the computer. Jon sat right down and turned it on. Chandler looked over his shoulder. "He said it only works for a few minutes at a time, so you have to do this quickly," Chandler advised, quietly, urgently.

"Right." But Jon really had no idea what that "this" was — Sasha had left no instructions in her little note. He supposed he could call or text her — he had her contact info in his phone. Jon looked at the screen. No, that probably wouldn't be necessary. As the icons popped into place, Jon noticed a shimmering new gift-wrapped box on the screen, named "Sasha's present."

Jon hesitated for a moment. He wasn't thrilled about doing this in front of Chandler. But he had no choice at this point, and Chandler could still be of help if the program proved balky.

Chandler saw the icon on the screen and pointed to it. Jon nodded, and clicked.

The screen that came up said: "Pay for anything you like online with any of your credit cards, and let my present do its work for you. You won't notice anything different immediately, but watch for what is on your bill — or not on your bill." And the words were followed by an animated little smiley icon.

"Good, that seems to be it," Chandler said nervously but happily. "Now just drag it to trash—"

But Jon went instead to his favorite online wine store. He had a strong feeling he and Trudi would soon have something to celebrate.

Jon 2

The slightly different universe...

Jon moved to shut off his computer, but got a chime from his email that he had a new message. It was a receipt for purchase of a bottle of Black Dirt Red Wine from Warwick. He and Trudi loved it — a great $12 wine they'd discovered at a farmer's market in the Fall — but why would Trudi buy a bottle now? They still had two bottles in their little rack the last time he'd looked — which had been maybe two days ago.

He called Trudi. "Nope, I didn't buy it," she told him. "I don't mind another bottle, though — maybe some grateful student bought it for you as a present. You really shouldn't accept it, I know. Or maybe some Dean wanted to thank you."

"I doubt if it's either," Jon said. "I don't see how either could have gotten my credit card."

"Yeah, that's right," Trudi said. "But then—"

"No big deal," Jon lied. "All right, I'm on my way home — anything I should pick up? We ok with orange juice and milk?"

Jon got off the phone with a grocery order and a thought that rang as painfully clear as day in his brain: this *was* a very big deal. He got up, paced around, and tried to find some balance on this. A credit card in his name for a bottle of wine he hadn't bought. The price was indeed no problem, but the process surely was. Maybe this was just some sort of credit card error? Jon smiled, ruefully. No, he knew that it wasn't. This was likely just what his alter-self had been going through. And now Jon in that parallel universe, the Jon who had been receiving this Jon's charges, had turned the tables.

Jon hoped his counterpart would continue to be this sparing with the charges. Jon certainly had not been with his. Was there a way this program could be disabled?

Jon 1

Our universe...

"No!" Chandler cried out, and lunged at Jon's computer. But Jon had already clicked on the wine. He had set this online store for express, one-click purchase, so he could get in a last-minute order when he was late for class.

Jon stood and restrained Chandler.

The techie stuck his head in the door. "It's ok," Jon said. "We're just rehearsing for a departmental play."

The techie looked at Jon and Chandler as if they were both crazy, but didn't see enough of a problem to warrant his continued intrusion. He walked back into his room.

Jon's computer promptly went off.

"You used that program to charge something to your alter-self?" Chandler demanded in a tremulous voice. "That's not right."

"No, it is," Jon said. "Here, have a seat. Let me explain what I think is going on."

Chandler looked at the computer as if to confirm it was off, and could do no further harm, then sat.

"I think I've been a victim of my alter-self's charges for several months now," Jon explained. "I don't know if there's any way I can undo them, now. But I can rectify this by charging my counterpart back.

Jon 2

The slightly different universe...

Jon shut his computer off, patted it, almost affectionately, regretfully, and headed for the door.

So this would be it. His computer, Sasha's extraordinary little program, had done well for him. But now that his counterpart in the parallel universe had finally gotten a clue about this, there was really no point in continuing. If each charge that this Jon shunted to the parallel Jon was matched by a charge from the parallel Jon to this Jon, there would be no net gain for either Jon. One Jon of course could make bigger charges, and charge more frequently, than the other Jon. But the other Jon would know this as soon as the trans-universe charges arrived, and could easily retaliate. So the net gain, sooner or later, would be zero. All that escalating charges in both universes could eventually engender would be mutually assured bankruptcy.

Jon got into his Prius and drove out of the university parking lot. This had been one wild ride, no doubt. Financial transactions across alternate universes. Had other pairs of parallel people being doing this? Had they started like Jon, with one doing it to the other, and then the other catching on? He still wondered why it had taken his parallel Jon so long to get going on this. He wondered if there was any way he could yet turn this back around to his own advantage, or at least prevent his alternate from transferring any more charges.

Where did the program, the technology, come from? Jon had heard rumors, conspiracy theories, about parallel universes, for years. Pathways to alternate realities brought into being by fast-moving quantum particles. Hypothetical informational superluminary highways. He passed by another Prius that looked like his, entering the parking lot, and sighed...

Sasha was the key to this. Her program made this real. He owed her a call. No point doing this in the car, though. He wanted to concentrate, take notes, if needed. There could be a career-making paper in this, for him as well as Sasha.

Jon 1

Our universe...

Jon turned the computer back on, on impulse. It made some strange noises, but stayed dark. He banged the table hard. "I wanted to see if I could get it to do it again," he said to Chandler.

The bang brought the dour techie back in. He shook his head. "I told you, it only stays up a few minutes. Banging the table won't change that."

"I know," Jon said. "Sorry. Could you see if you could get it working again now, even if for just a few minutes?"

Chandler, who obviously had been struggling with how to react to this, finally spoke. "Yes," he said to the techie, "if you could do that, it would be very helpful. He has notes for a new paper on that computer, which he doesn't have anyplace else, and lots of people are eager to see it."

Jon nodded and smiled at Chandler, grateful for the support.

"I'd like to see those notes myself," Chandler added.

The techie grunted, motioned Jon out of his seat, and got to work on the computer. He put in four different diagnostic and boot disks. None had any effect. The techie frowned. "It may be permanently brain dead," he said. "I can have someone else look at it, but usually when these things are gone they're gone."

"But—" Jon started, but realized there was not much more it was safe to tell this guy. Letting him know that this half or completely dead computer contained some extraordinary program was a sure ticket to the techie saying any repair was futile, and keeping the computer for himself. "Ok, thanks for trying," Jon said. "No need to do anything more about this now. Could you pack it up for me so I can take back to—"

The techie shook his head no. "Lots of reasons I can't do that. You need a form signed by the Chair of your Department. I'm about to pack up and leave — closing the shop early today, I have an appointment."

"Ok," Jon knew all about the forms, and how intractable the techies were about requiring them. The money would be deducted from their salaries, maybe worse, if any computer went missing. "Thanks," Jon said. "I'll see if I can come back with the signed form tomorrow — that ok?" Best Jon could do — his Chair was in Manhattan today.

The techie made an I-don't-care face.

"Thanks," Jon said, again.

He and Chandler left the building. Ordinarily, Jon would have complained about the repair facility closing early, it would have driven him a little crazy, but not today. Let the techie shut down the room and go to his appointment. With a new set of broken computers to deal with tomorrow, the techie would likely not give Jon's computer another thought. And then Jon could get his computer, and try to find someone who could get it to work.

Meanwhile, the best thing to do now, Jon considered, was call Sasha. Maybe it was the best thing in any case. If she could send him another copy of her program that Jon could install on a fresh computer, that would take care of everything. He didn't see why she wouldn't send it to him.

But he didn't want to call Sasha right in front of Chandler. He started to thank Chandler, and say he had to be getting home.

"But there's a lot more I'd like to know about this," Chandler objected, "a lot more we need to discuss."

"I know," Jon said. "But I can't do it now." Not before he spoke to Sasha. With no evidence in hand, Chandler couldn't do much, not anything really, with what he had just seen. Anyone other than Jon and Sasha would dismiss Chandler as a nutcase if he'd try to inform them about what he thought had just happened.

They approached the garage. "Can I give you a lift to the train?" Jon asked Chandler, in a bid to get him off campus and as far away from the computer as soon as possible.

Chandler was clearly still not happy about the way this day was concluding, but he accepted the offer. "Sure, thanks."

Jon dropped him off at the Metro-North, and swung over to the parkway. He'd call Sasha as soon as he got home and gave Trudi a long hug.

Eugene 2

The slightly different universe...

Eugene had been keeping an eye on the lab from a safe distance down the corridor. As soon as Jon left, Eugene went right over to Jon's computer. He turned it on, called up the program Sasha had left Jon, and then the program Sasha had left on Jon's computer for Eugene. He smiled broadly.

He skyped Sasha. "I think we can move on to our next couplet now," Eugene told her. "The Jons seem to have reached their equilibrium."

"Good," Sasha said. "Took the Jon in the other universe long enough."

"Yeah, we need to look into that, could be an important data point," Eugene said. "The ginger ale on the keyboard was of course my doing — part of our protocol for seeing what happens when real life throws in a monkey wrench. But I can't figure why the computer techie was taking so long."

"Could be another monkey wrench — unexpected — could be he ran some diagnostic and found something unusual about our program," Sasha said.

"It's supposed to be self-disguising to the usual scans."

"I know. You should get the computer out of his hands in any case," Sasha said.

"Yeah, the tech center should be closing in under an hour. That'll be my next stop today," Eugene said.

"Good."

"Meanwhile, you proceeding well with your Professor Ramapuram out there in California?" Eugene asked.

"Yah," Sasha nodded.

"Excellent," Eugene said. "I've been accepted as his grad assistant in the Fall. You leave him the code at the end of this term, and move on to another school. I'll come out there to keep watch and we'll be in business, just as with Jon and the others."

"Jon will likely be calling me, to get a little more clarity on what's been happening to him."

Eugene laughed. "Tell him the usual. You stumbled on to this program with the quantum mechanical app, wasn't really sure what it could do, so you left it in his wiser hands. Give him your heartfelt apology for not telling him more upfront. He'd need a nova of light to understand what's really happening — hey, we're not much better, are we?"

"But I'll shut him down, tell him the program is unstable, that I need to do much more work on it before I set it loose again — give to anyone as a present," Sasha said.

"Right," Eugene said, and got thoughtful. "You think our alternates, Eugene and Sasha in the parallel universe, are having something like this same conversation right now?"

Now Sasha smiled. "I'll do you one better: You think there may be another group of happy researchers, much like us, in yet another parallel universe, and they're running us, testing our responses, just as we've been doing with the Jons?"

THE WALLET

First published in The Sci Phi Journal, *February 2015.*

My phone rang. I put it to my ear.

"Professor Klein?"

"Yes?" I had just taken off my coat, put on the water for tea, and the last person I wanted to hear from was Lauren from the office, as much as I generally liked her and her hardworking attitude.

"I thought you'd be relieved to know I have your wallet right here."

"My wallet?" I hadn't known that I'd lost it. Good thing I hadn't given into my impulse to speed on the way home.

"Yep, it's right here," she said again. "I found it myself," she added proudly, "right by the elevator. It has your photo ID, driver's license, card from your town pool—"

"Ok, thanks a million — I'll be there in fifteen minutes." That's what I got for being too lazy to run down the stairs.

I put my phone back in my pants pocket and grabbed my jacket. I felt a familiar bulge in each pocket of my jacket as I put it on. One was my voluminous set of keys, which always made me feel like a janitor. The other was . . . my wallet.

***

I took it out and looked at it. Yep, it was my wallet.

Now I knew that Lauren wasn't the kind of person to be playing some practical joke on me. She was thirty-six, mother of two sweet little kids, and had been with the English Department for almost a decade. No point in calling her back and telling her I had my wallet right in my hand. I might as well take the fifteen-minute drive on the parkway and see what was going on.

Maybe the Department was throwing me some kind of surprise party for an award which I hadn't yet been notified about. I should be so lucky. And, besides, why would Lauren make up a story about my losing my wallet to get me back to the office? Lots of easier ways to do that, like saying a colleague or a student had come by with an urgent need to see me.

It took me twenty-two minutes to get to the school this time, thanks to some new construction on the highway which slowed everything up. I parked the car and walked into Larraby Hall. Henry, the usual security guard, wasn't there. Someone I had seen a few times, but I didn't know his name, smiled and waved me through. I walked quickly up the three flights of stairs to my Department's offices.

"Where's Lauren?" I asked the student worker — I think her name was Elizabeth — who was sitting behind Lauren's desk.

"Oh, her little boy was rushed to the hospital — appendicitis, but he's ok," Elizabeth assured me.

"Good," I said. This seemed to be a day for out-of-the-blue bad luck, but at least Lauren's son was all right. "Did Lauren leave anything for—"

"Yes!" Elizabeth said. "Sorry, I should have told you as soon as you walked in. She said she was going to leave it with Henry, you know, the security guard downstairs?"

***

I thanked Elizabeth and walked slowly back into the hall. This all hung on Lauren. I believed I knew her well enough to know that she wasn't playing some sort of game with me. What would she have to gain by calling me at home, lying about having my wallet, getting me to come down here, and then playing the additional game of lying to Elizabeth about her boy being sick, and cleverly saying she would leave the wallet with Henry, when she knew he wasn't there? But if she wasn't lying for whatever motive, what then?

Was Lauren suffering from some sort of psychotic breakdown, which made her believe that she had my wallet, and her boy was sick, and all of that? That was hard to believe, too. Could it have been someone else's wallet that she'd found? She'd said it had had my photo ID, which would mean she was flat-out lying or crazy if the wallet had belonged to another professor or some student.

But if she wasn't lying and hadn't lost her mind about my losing my wallet, what was going on here? It almost was easier to believe that I had indeed lost my wallet, and Lauren had found it, except when I patted my jacket pocket, my wallet was right there. I took it out and looked at it again.

It looked no different. I examined its contents. I usually had a pretty good idea of how much cash I had. Twenty-four dollars, if memory served. I had started the day with three ten-dollar bills, but had paid five dollars plus tax for a turkey and cheddar sandwich, which left me with two ten-dollar bills and four one-dollar bills, which was exactly what was in my wallet right now, in addition to the change in my pocket. My credit cards, school ID, driver's license and all of that seemed right where they should be, too.

All right, so that confirmed — maybe — that someone hadn't pickpocketed my real wallet, and left me with this one, and then dropped my real wallet by the elevator after removing the cash and credit cards. Except why on Earth would someone single me out to do that, at a university no less? I hadn't a clue. A disgruntled student? Nah, I'd given everyone Bs and As last term. Hey, they'd been bright students.

I sighed, and decided to see if the security guard downstairs knew anything about this, or about Henry, before I headed home.
***

The guard was still amiable, but professed to know nothing about what was going on. "Sure, I know Henry, but I didn't see him today. Tonight is my shift."

"Ok, and Lauren — our department secretary — didn't leave a package with you?" I asked.

He shook his head no.

"Ok, thanks," I said and walked out of the building to the parking lot. I tried to recall if I'd seen Henry, or any security guard, the last time I'd left this building today, right after I'd allegedly dropped my wallet by the elevator upstairs. Maddeningly, I couldn't recall. I remembered a group of maintenance guys crowded around the security podium — they often did that, talking about sports, politics, whatever — but I couldn't see in my recollection who actually had been standing at the podium.

The ride home took more than thirty minutes. The construction was even worse. "Hey," my wife said when I opened the door. "Is everything ok? You're a little later than usual — I just got home. I was about to call you."

"Traffic," I replied, partially truthfully. I'd gotten so caught up in the wallet that I hadn't called her. And now that this whole thing seemed even more insane, I decided maybe there was no point in telling her what had happened. She was already on my case about being an absent-minded professor, and why upset her about something which I couldn't explain even to myself.

I put it mostly out of my mind, and went upstairs to shower and change into something more comfortable. We had an early dinner, watched a little television, and went to bed.

***

I had a class to teach early the next morning. I kissed my wife, made sure I had my wallet, and got into the car. The construction had spread, the drive was even longer, but fortunately I'd left early enough to get to class on time.

I walked to my office after the class — the office and the class were on opposite sides of the campus, story of my life — and girded myself for meeting Lauren. I stopped in the cafe on the ground floor and ordered another turkey and cheddar sandwich to eat later, for lunch. I like what I like, and they sometimes ran out of them.

There was yet a third security guard at his post — still not Henry and not the other guy — and sitting behind Lauren's desk upstairs was another student assistant, Tiffany. "Where's Lauren?" I asked.

"She's in the hospital with her son," Tiffany replied. "Appendicitis, he's ok. I'll be here for most of the day, and

Elizabeth will be in later."

"Of course," I said, "thanks." I went to my office.

I turned on my desktop. I liked looking at my email that way, rather than on the cramped phone. I scanned through my Inbox. There was a message waiting from Lauren. It was date-stamped yesterday — well before the dozen or so more emails that had arrived since then. Gmail sometimes does that, doesn't it? Yeah, I'd received messages hours or more after they'd been sent, before. Irritating, but, hey, you get what you pay for with Gmail.

I opened Lauren's email. It was time stamped about five minutes before she had called me yesterday. It said, "Professor Klein, I found your wallet by the elevator! It has eighteen dollars in cash, and lots of credit cards and IDs. I'm going to call you now and let you know, but I wanted to send you this email, in case I couldn't get through for some reason." I pulled out my wallet. My turkey and cheddar sandwich, which was now staring at me from the desk and suddenly didn't look very appetizing, had cost me the same five dollars and change as it had yesterday. I'd started the day with twenty-four dollars in my wallet — two ten-dollar bills and four singles. I had paid for my sandwich today with a ten-dollar bill, and had received back four singles and change. That left one ten-dollar bill, and eight singles in my wallet — or exactly what Lauren had said in her email was in there yesterday, after she had found my wallet by the elevator. How could she have known yesterday what was in my wallet today, when the amount of money I had in my wallet was more yesterday than today, because I had purchased that sandwich today?

I had another class late in the morning, and a bunch of student appointments, but I couldn't get what was in my wallet out of my mind. At one point, I removed the ten-dollar bill and put it in my desk — would that change what Lauren had written in her email about what was in my wallet, because now there were in fact only eight single-dollar bills? Was there some sort of quantum mechanical, mystical, or whatever unfathomable connection between what I had in my wallet and what Lauren had seen in my wallet yesterday? I'm no physicist, but I had read somewhere that some theories of quantum mechanics said that what you were thinking could influence the position of particles — but that influence couldn't extend to money in wallets across time, could it?

No, I closed the drawer with the ten-dollar bill, and Lauren's email on my screen was still the same, telling me she'd seen eighteen dollars in my wallet, not eight. I took the ten-dollar bill out of the desk and put it back in my wallet — I had already proven something, that my actions now had no influence on what Lauren had emailed to me, so no point in divesting myself of the ten dollars—

Wait. If I put the ten-dollar bill back in my wallet, that would remove the "proof" that my actions here had no influence on what Lauren had told me, because I would still have the eighteen dollars in my wallet. But—

I went through this several times, shuttling the ten-dollar bill between my wallet and desk drawer, and finally decided to leave the damn ten dollars in my desk. That seemed a better way to demonstrate whatever the hell I was trying to demonstrate. One thing I was sure of: her email on my screen from yesterday was exactly the same. It still said that she had seen eighteen dollars in my wallet yesterday, even though I didn't have that amount until today, and even when I had just repeatedly taken ten dollars out of the eighteen dollars my wallet and put that ten-dollar bill into my desk drawer.

Thinking more about her email, I suppose it was possible that she was a master hacker, or a master hacker had gotten into her account, and had sent the email mentioning the eighteen dollars to me today — after I had purchased my sandwich with the result that I had just eighteen dollars in my wallet — but had date-stamped the email last night. But in addition to the fact that I highly doubted she was a hacker at all, how could she have known this morning that I had even purchased the sandwich? I hadn't seen her in the cafe. Was someone else in the cafe spying on me for some reason, had seen me purchase the sandwich, and was also a genius hacker or in touch with one? Even if that were the case, there was no way that person would know how much money I had left in my wallet — even the cashier, a woman in her twenties, couldn't have known that.

At some point in the afternoon I looked again at my turkey and cheddar sandwich. I was hungry. I picked it up and took a bite. I felt like I was eating some kind of cosmically significant evidence, but I consumed it all, anyway.   After I finished the sandwich, I realized what it apparently was evidence of: leaving my money in the desk had no effect on what Lauren had seen in my wallet the day before, but spending my money on the sandwich did. But what did that mean?   Some kind of quantum mechanics at work in a sandwich?

It was getting time for me to go home. I felt my wallet in my pocket. I was going to hold on to it for dear life.

I walked by the secretary's office and stuck my head in.

"Professor Klein!" a cheery voice said. It was Lauren's, she was behind her desk now.

***

I didn't know what to say, where to begin. "Hey—" I began

Lauren's phone rang. She put it to her ear, nodded slowly, and looked a little upset. "Hi honey, you have an upset tummy?"

'It's my little boy, Kenny,' she mouthed to me. 'Babysitter called and said he has an upset stomach.'

"Ok, sweetie," she said back to the phone, "here's a little kiss from Mommy over the phone." She made a big noisy kiss. "I'll be home soon. Let me speak to Janny, ok? Mommy loves you."

Janny was presumably the baby-sitter. "Ok," Lauren said to her. "Is Tom all right? Good! Ok, I'll be home soon."
Tom was two years older than Kenny, if memory served.

Lauren put down the phone, and looked at me. "I'm sorry—" she said

"No, no," I assured her. "Family comes first. You should go home now." But should I tell her that Kenny had an appendix that would need attention in the hospital? Could I even be sure that that's what was happening? Elizabeth had said that Lauren had left the office yesterday — Elizabeth had told me that yesterday, not today — and I guess the implication was Lauren had received that call here, in the office.

"I will," Lauren was saying, "I just need to get these resumes uploaded to Folio for the departmental search."

I considered what to say next — should I tell her about her call to me yesterday? — when Owens, the Chair of the Department, strode into the office with a stack of paperwork and laborious instructions for Lauren. I waited quietly on the side until he finished, but he was aware of my presence and apparently wasn't thrilled about it.

"Can I help you with anything?" he asked.

"Ah, no, that's ok," I said and left. I never liked the guy.

I returned to my office, and decided I'd done enough here for the day. I put on my jacket, clutched my wallet, walked by Lauren's office, and waved goodbye. Owens was still boring her with a long harangue about something.

I walked past the security guard — again, not Henry — out into the street and down the pathway to my car. I felt my wallet again. I definitely had not dropped it by the elevator.

There was even more construction than before on the parkway — it seemed to be growing each time I drove by — and there were two cop cars and several police on hand. What was going on here? This seemed to be something more than just construction.

I stopped by one of the police cars, rolled down a window, and pulled out my wallet with my university ID. I'd found over the years that it never hurt to show it to police when you wanted their help. The cop opened the door of his car and eyed my ID. "You need to move on professor. We can't have people congregating here."

"Of course," I said. "But can you just tell me what happened?"

"Someone was behind the wheel, not paying attention. Drove right into the construction." He pointed to a car, steaming from its open hood.

"And—"

Another officer walked up to the cop in the car I was talking to. He turned to me. "You can't stay here," the second cop said.

"Ok," I said and pulled my car back onto the parkway. I arrived home about ten minutes later. It was pretty much the same time I had arrived home yesterday. I took my jacket off, and put on a pot of water for tea.

My phone rang.

"Professor Klein?"

Damn, it was Lauren. "Yes?"

"I thought you'd be relieved to know I have your wallet right here."

"I'll be right down," I said, very slowly. Then, on impulse, "how's your boy, Kenny?"

"Oh, he's no worse, as far as I know," Lauren replied. "It's nice of you to ask, Professor. I was just leaving, when I found your wallet — by the elevator."

"Thanks so much," I said. "One quick question — can you look and tell me how much cash is in the wallet?"

She laughed in an odd way. "You want to make sure no one took any of it? Given what students have to pay for textbooks these days, I don't blame you." She laughed, nervously, again.

"No, yes, thanks," I said, a little incoherently. "And I of course know that you didn't take any."

"Eight dollars," Lauren said. "You have eight dollars in your wallet, all singles."

"Thanks so much," I said again. "I'll be right down."

***

I put on my jacket and instinctively patted my pocket and removed the wallet which I knew would be there — the very same wallet, apparently and insanely, that Lauren had just convincingly told me she was holding in her hand, once again. But not the same wallet which Lauren had called and emailed me about yesterday, which had contained eighteen dollars. Today that wallet, impossibly both in my hand and at the same time in Lauren's hands some fifteen miles down the parkway, contained eight dollars. I looked at the eight dollars in the wallet in my hand and tried to comprehend what I was seeing. Leaving the ten-dollar bill in my desk apparently did influence what Lauren was seeing in her alternate universe or whatever it was, just not immediately. Or maybe leaving the money in my desk had no effect at first because I was still in the room and could easily remove it, which in fact I had done more than once.

I left voicemail for my wife that I would be home late and got in the car. I was feeling like I was in *Groundhog Day*, that movie in which Bill Murray lived the same day over and over again, except this wasn't quite like that, either. Each of my days had had a different class schedule, just as they should have in my world, before it became unhinged. And I didn't recall the same object being in two different places at the same time in that movie, either. And — more importantly — this wasn't a damn movie, it was my life. I took a quick look at the calendar on my phone. It was the 4th of March, which was definitely a day later than yesterday, March 3rd. I was not in a time loop, not a one-day time loop, anyway. Whatever I was in, it was something different.

There were even more cop cars around the construction site this time, but I didn't stop to ask questions. This worsening situation on the parkway maybe had some significance to what was going on with me and my wallet, I realized, but I couldn't even begin to figure out what that might be. Wallets, sandwiches, money, parkways, all mixed up in some kind of crazy jumble of reality — it was too much to grasp, some warped indigestible food for thought.

I parked my car in the school lot and hustled to my building. Yet a fourth guard — not Henry, not the guy from yesterday, not the guy from earlier today — was at the post. I ran up the three flights of stairs to my department's offices.

Elizabeth was sitting again at Lauren's desk. But she looked more serious than yesterday.

"Is Lauren?—" I began, out of breath.

"Her little boy was rushed to the hospital with appendicitis," Elizabeth said. "They got him there just in time — my cousin's appendix burst before they got him to the hospital a few years ago. He almost died!"

"But Kenny — Lauren's little boy — is ok? They got him to the hospital in time?"

"Yeah," Elizabeth said. "Oh, I'm sorry — you came about your wallet, right? Lauren said she'd leave it for you with Henry the security guard downstairs. He didn't give it to you when you walked in?"

"No," I said. "That's ok." I smiled and reassured her. No point in further distressing her by telling her that Henry hadn't been at his post for two days, bizarrely linked in some way to my wallet and whatever the hell was going on here.

I left, dazed, and walked slowly down the stairs. I'd been thinking of going to my office and removing the ten-dollar bill and seeing what eventually happened, but I was too upset to pursue that petty experimentation. Whatever was occurring was now putting people in dire jeopardy, sending Lauren's boy to the hospital with a ruptured or nearly ruptured appendix.

I did check with the security guard just to make sure nothing had been left for me, and of course he shook his head no.

I got in my car for the drive home.

***

My best honest explanation and maybe biggest fear at this point about what was happening is that I was the one who must have had some kind of psychotic breakdown, not Lauren. I could see a shrink tomorrow, but how would I know if I was really seeing the shrink or if that visit was just another part of my psychotic delusion? Actually, I realized that my being crazy was definitely not my biggest fear — all of this really happening would be far worse, whatever exactly "really" meant in this case.

I tried to think. How could I get out of this? I seemed to have some power to influence events, but only insofar as the amount of cash in my wallet, and not in a way that made any sense.

I approached the construction site on the parkway. Even more cops. This time I stopped, and encountered a sergeant. I showed her my school ID and asked what was happening.

She looked at me strangely. "I can't really talk about this, but I'll tell you that someone from your school — a security guard — crashed into this construction. I'm sorry to tell you he lost his life."

My God! "Was his name Henry?"

The sergeant nodded. "I really can't say any more. I'm very sorry for your loss."

I pulled my car back on to the roadway and tried to collect my thoughts. I just knew I was somehow responsible for this — for Henry's death, for Lauren's son being rushed to the hospital. But how? Why?

The only thing that really mattered immediately was what could I do about it. An idea popped into my head. Matter and anti-matter. Didn't they annihilate everything around them if they came together? I didn't know for sure. I was no scientist. But I saw that in a movie somewhere, or a television show, or maybe I'd read it in a story.

The only thing I seemed to have any control over was my wallet, sometimes. I had to go back to that. Maybe this insanity — including Henry's death now — was triggered by my wallet somehow being in two different places at the same time. That wasn't my fault. But … maybe I could do something about it. The universe had bifurcated for some reason around my wallet. The universe had torn itself in half, and people were suffering. But maybe I could do something to heal it. Maybe that would save Henry.

I got off at the next exit and made my way to the Hudson River. I parked and walked slowly to the dock. I had power over my wallet. Maybe if I was the one to make it disappear, that would burst this bubble from hell. That should certainly have more of an effect than how much money I had in the wallet, and whether I used it to buy a stupid turkey sandwich, right?

This was only a theory, but what would it hurt to try it? The loss of my wallet would be slight compared to the loss of a life.

I could throw my wallet into the river. It would likely never be seen again. And— no, I could do even better. I could burn my wallet, and throw the ashes out into the river. And that would leave just one of my wallets left in my world — the one back in my office. That lunatic act might be all that was needed to make the universe whole and sane again.

I walked back to my car, where I still had a lighter and fluid from a decade ago, when I used to smoke. It was a crazy thing to do, to destroy my wallet like this. I knew that. But I doused the wallet, lit the paper bills and then the edges of the wallet and watched it burn. I picked up the ashes with a piece of cardboard on the ground and threw it all over the railing into the darkly gleaming river below. I consoled myself with the thought that hey, at least I wasn't throwing myself into that chilly water.

***

I got home, had a quick dinner with my wife, and pled that I was coming down with something. I went upstairs to bed. I thought, maybe I am getting a little crazy but if that's what it took to stop the craziness that had suddenly jumped up all around me then that would be worth it. And, amazingly, I fell right asleep.

My wife was gone when I awoke the next day — I had slept like a baby, and really late, into the afternoon. I found a note saying I should go to the doctor if I was feeling any worse, and she loved me. But I was feeling well rested and great. I did feel a little guilty that I hadn't told her about this, but I was mostly relieved that, if my eradication of my wallet had worked, then she would be beyond any danger of what had happened to poor Henry.

I had no classes, but there was always something to do in my office, and I had to see what was going on there today. I ate a quick breakfast and got in my car.

No construction was on the highway! I interpreted that as a good sign, though I knew full well that Henry could still have been killed, and the police investigation and the construction itself had concluded. I'd know more when I got to school.

There was a group of maintenance workers around the security post but no Henry. "He's in the john," one of the workers told me. I didn't have the heart to ask who "he" was. I just nodded and bounded up the stairs.

Lauren was at her desk, and all smiles! "Professor Klein! I was wondering why you didn't come in for this." She handed me an envelope with my wallet inside.

I took it and put it in my pocket. "Thank you!" I said with a big smile.

I considered going into my office, but I realized that in order to see if I was free of this, I would have to drive home. "Oh — I just realized I have to take care of something at home — our gardener's coming by," I lied to Lauren. "I'll see you tomorrow. And thanks again!"

"Sure!"

I started walking out, then turned around. "Your family all doing great?" I asked.

"Absolutely," Lauren replied. "It's very nice of you to ask."

"As my grandmother always told me, if you have your health you have your wealth," I said with a flourish and left.

I walked down the stairs. Henry was behind the security post!

"Hey!" I said, and shook his hand.

"Having a good day Professor?" he asked.

"The best!" I replied. I stopped in the cafe and bought a turkey cheddar sandwich.

I got in my car. Still no construction on the highway. The ride took fifteen minutes, as it had on the way down.

Damn, this just may have worked! Either my psychotic episode had passed, or I had cut through this sick quantum entanglement or whatever it was by getting rid of my other wallet. I didn't understand all the warped rules here, all the natural or unnatural laws, by any means, if at all, but maybe I'd gotten enough of it right to change the deadly game. Matter and anti-matter — I had removed one of those toxic components from this harrowing equation. I'd cut out the tumor.

I got home, took off my jacket, and turned on the tea kettle.

I realized that I hadn't checked my wallet to see how much cash it contained—

And the phone rang.

I froze. Was this Lauren?

"Hello?" I asked in a choked voice.

"Sweetheart? Can't talk, but I just wanted to make sure you were ok."

It was my wife. "Yes!" I threw her a kiss. "I'm fine! Feeling much better."

"Great!" she said. "How about I bring home something good to eat for dinner tonight?"

"How about we go out to Taverna?" It was our favorite restaurant. "I have some things I want to tell you about."

"You're in a celebratory mood," she said.

"I am," I said. "Life is good."

"Love you," she said, and we got off the phone.

Life was indeed good, at least now. The tea kettle whistled. The phone rang again.

"Hi honey—" I began.

Uneasy laughter on the phone. "Professor Klein? I thought you'd be relieved to know that I have your wallet here. I found it by the elevator. It has three dollars in it."

SLIPPING TIME

First published in Amazing Stories, *August 2018.*

I slipped on the wet pavement. I got to my feet and soon discovered it was five hours earlier. This was not the first time this had happened – I knew all the signs. My phone was not broken, it was really five hours earlier. The newspaper on the ground confirmed it: The paper was bone dry, even though it had been raining cats and dogs, or big sloppy drops, anyway, where I had just been, right here, a split second ago.

I returned to her apartment – fortunately, about fifteen minutes after I had left, five hours earlier. I was grateful for the second chance.

"You're wet," she said and invited me in. "Someone throw a bucket of water on you?"

"Something like that," I said, with an embarrassed smile.

She took a towel out of her linen closet and tossed it to me.

"Thanks," I said. "Look, I'm sorry – I was stupid earlier."

"You were," she said. "But I accept your apology." She put her arms around me and kissed me.

Her body felt good next to mine ... but I knew we couldn't stay here long enough to take full advantage of this. If I recalled correctly, my earlier self was due to return in just a few minutes – hell, who was I kidding, of course I remembered correctly, my earlier self was due to return in a few minutes just five hours ago from where I had been this afternoon in the pouring rain, and there was no way I could possibly forget what had happened that first time. Not something that had occurred so recently. Not if it had occurred five years or even decades ago.

I pulled slightly away and ran my finger over her lips. "You know what, I'm starving. How about we get some sushi and continue this later?" Neither of us had eaten lunch when I'd left in a huff the first time, so it was a good bet that she was hungry, too.

She agreed. I took her hand and we sprinted down the two flights of stairs to the street.

"Looks like rain," she said and looked up at the sky, which had grown puffy and grey since I'd walked up the stairs of her brownstone just a few minutes ago.

"Yeah, but not for a few hours," I said, squinting at the sky, then back into her eyes. "Probably."

She gave me a slightly strange look, and squeezed my hand.

The sushi restaurant was just a block away, but had no line of sight to her brownstone, which was just what I wanted. Last thing I needed was my earlier self catching a glimpse of me now, throwing him and me into an infinite regress paradox, as we both suddenly recalled the incident, and struggled to make sense of the ricocheting mirrors of memory in our minds. That had happened to me once, a few years ago, and I'd been out of commission, a veritable vegetable, for weeks after that.

The weather was still nice, and, since I indeed knew, from first-hand experience, that it would not start raining until at least four hours from now, we sat outdoors and looked over the sushi menus on our table.

The fatty tuna and sweet shrimp that we ordered looked delicious, but I was actually more interested in the waiter who approached with two cups of green tea. Back in Vanessa's apartment – I guess it can't hurt for you to know her name, how many long-necked women named Vanessa must there be in New York, hundreds maybe, right? – but back in her apartment, in the previous reality, the tea had coincided with, maybe triggered, that argument. I had slipped on a piece of paper as I walked with two cups of tea towards Vanessa at the table, and a little spilled on her. Fortunately I hadn't fallen to the floor, so no time disruption had ensued. But let's face it, the fight had been about something much more serious than tea, and—

Our waiter placed his two cups of tea perfectly in front of each of us, bowed, and receded. I had noticed that there were certain resonances, echoes, whatever you want to call them, in the various realities I visited, or, who knows, maybe engendered with my time slips. But none regarding the two sets of tea in the previously reality and this one, where the tea in each of the cups now sat still as night and shimmering on the table. I lifted mine, sipped, and looked at Vanessa.

"You look like there's something you want to tell me," she said, slowly lifting and sipping from her cup.

"Do I?" I asked. "And what does that look like? That look?"

Vanessa smiled. There was probably no other woman in New York of any name with lips curved that way. She took my hand and spoke softly. "I already more than accepted your apology. So it's not that. There's something else on your mind."

I started to deny that, but of course she was right. I realized that a part of me now wanted to tell her what had actually happened, and who this man sitting in front of her really was – no, that was too melodramatic, I was the same man – but I wanted to tell her that I was five hours older and wiser than the man she thought she knew. And, more, the reason I was actually five hours older.

The waiter arrived with our sushi. "Thank you," I said, and returned my full attention to Vanessa. She bit into a sweet shrimp. Her eyes half closed in pleasure.

I hated to spoil that expression. That was the least of the reasons I didn't want to say what I was thinking. But – "There's something I need to tell you."

She opened her eyes and looked at me, not the plate. "Professional or personal?"

"Personal," I replied. "But not what you might think. I'm not sleeping with anyone else."

She nodded slowly, apparently believing me. "Are you feeling ok?" she asked, with real concern.

"Yeah. Physically." I had to be very careful with what I said next – no slips of the tongue about time slips. Telling my lovers the truth about this had always busted my relationships, though maybe we were all destined to break up anyway. But no one wants to share a bed or even a kitchen table with a guy who thought he time traveled at, basically, the drop of a hat. Or said he time traveled in any manner. They thought I was crazy. I felt like I was crazy even thinking about this. But not talking about this, keeping it bottled up in my brain, had not worked too well, either.

Vanessa's brown eyes had narrowed. She put her hand over mine again. "What's the matter, baby?" Her fingers wrapped tightly around mine.

I sighed. "I–" Maybe this wasn't such a good idea.

"Tell me," she coaxed, gently.

"I didn't tell you why my hair was wet," I said.

"Someone really doused your head with water? That's what's bothering you?"
She clearly didn't believe that.

"My hair was wet because I had been walking in the rain."

She laughed, not particularly joyfully. "But it hasn't rained since you left."

"Right. It's going to rain in a few hours."

"So you're telling me, what, that you were thinking it was going to rain, and that's what got your hair wet – that's crazy." She withdrew her hand.

"No, that's not it. But what actually happened to me might be more crazy."

She waved away the re-approaching waiter. "Now you're scaring me a little. I don't understand."

I finished the last piece of sushi on the plate.

"Let's get the check," Vanessa said, suddenly, and waved back the same waiter. "We probably should continue talking about this in more private surroundings."

I nodded, and quickly calculated. She no doubt meant her apartment. My earlier self had almost certainly come back already, found no one at home, and gone about his business. Whatever that business may have been. I had no idea what he did after he left Vanessa's brownstone, because that was no longer me. He was no longer me. He was part of Reality 1, and I was in Reality 2, and the branching had occurred the instant I had slipped on the wet sidewalk. Actually, there were far more realities stacked up in my strange existence, but today, fortunately, there had been just one.

Therefore, so far, there were just two realities – with me, from Reality 1, now in Reality 2, five hours before the slip, and he, also from Reality 1, now continuing in Reality 1 at this exact same parallel time, up until the slip in time. The key was making sure the two realities didn't intersect. At least, that's how I thought it worked. But what the hell did I know? I only lived it, that certainly was no reason I would understand it correctly.

The check arrived. I put a $20 bill on the table, then a five, to give the waiter even a better tip. For some reason, I was in a better mood.

I noted it still looked like rain, but of course the rain hadn't yet started, when we left the restaurant.

Vanessa took my arm. Neither of us said anything as we walked back to her apartment. I was relieved not to find myself loitering around in front of her building. We quickly climbed the stairs.

She whirled around and started kissing me as soon we entered her apartment and closed the door. I put my hands on the small of her back and moved them down. She unbuttoned my shirt, I unbuckled her belt, and we were soon in her bed without any clothes.

It was ironic, I thought, as her legs wrapped around my back and I played with her tongue, that we wouldn't be here like this right now if I hadn't time slipped several months ago after that party. I'd never taken advantage of a time slip like that before, usually it had the reverse effect on my love life, like it had been having for most of today.

There had been a chemistry between us at the party, for sure, but I was slow on the uptake and she'd left with some other people before I'd even gotten her number. But she had mentioned that she'd just landed a job at the university as an adjunct, and when I slipped in time two days later to a week before, I figured, hey, it was worth a shot. I hung out in the Starbucks just off campus a few times and got lucky on the third try. I struck up a conversation, we had a cup of coffee, and the rest, as they say, is history.

Well, as much as anyone could speak of history in my... condition. The thing is, I had no control over when I slipped. I couldn't deliberately slip on something and travel back in time – it was always back in time, by the way, never ahead, to the future. It was fall back, never spring ahead, like Daylight Saving Time. But for the slip to be a slip in time, I had to slip in a truly accidental way –

I felt her body cleaving to mine. Speaking of being beyond control, we were both just about there now. I had to say, this loss of control was a rush that felt much better than slipping in the street –

We were both half asleep, I guess, but I was awake enough to wonder if I should resume the conversation we'd been having in the sushi place, or maybe just let this slide. She made a contented noise. "How are you feeling now?" she asked. "Any better?"

So I guess we would be resuming our little talk. "Yeah," I said, and kissed her gently on the back of her neck.

We were spooning. She turned around and touched my face. "We were talking about the rain."

"Yeah," I repeated. "Sometimes, you know, I suddenly feel like I'm in a different time." I guess that was a good way to get back to the subject.

"You know, having sex makes me feel a little like that," she said.

"Yeah, I know what you mean, but I think what I'm feeling is different – like I'm actually in a different time."

"Seeing a different time or actually being in it?" she asked.

Her tone was still affectionate. This was the make or break point. I could soft pedal, blur what I had been saying, or –

"No, actually being there, actually moving back a few hours in time." I took the plunge. "Sometimes days, weeks." Thankfully it had never been more than that.

She stroked my face and kissed me. "What is time, really, anyway? It's in our heads, all subjective, right?"

"The rain on my head a little while from now wasn't just in my mind," I said. "You saw it. It was on my head, not in my head." I turned away from her and caught my breath. I was surprised that she wasn't frightened, like she was in the sushi place, and the last thing I wanted was to blow up her good mood, but I had gone too far down this path of true confession to turn around now.

"How does it happen," she asked, gently turning my face back to hers and apparently not perturbed, "your flipping back in time?"

"It happens when I accidentally slip and fall," I replied, "and not every time, not even most of the time."

"You are a little bit of a klutz," she said, playfully, and kissed me some more.

"I'm not clear if the physical slipping causes the time slip, or whether something triggers the time slip and makes me slip on the street –"

Her response was to put her arms around my body and pull me closer to her and she couldn't answer anyway because her mouth was on mine and then on my neck and chest and –

The second time was in some ways even better than the first, as it often is, and as we lay in each other's arms in the sweet, soft afterglow, I wondered again if I should resume the conversation. There was a part of my brain which was saying, enough already, forget about it, move on to other things, but I knew this wouldn't go away.

"Each time I slip back in time, I trigger a new reality, if that makes any sense," I said, tentatively.

"Mmm…" she said, maybe more asleep than awake.

I pressed on. "In the previous reality – before the one we're now in – we had a big argument."

"We had an argument in this one," she said, almost tenderly, "about your complaining that I hadn't bought any orange juice for you, and I already forgave you for that, remember?"

"Yeah, but there was a second argument, worse than the first," I replied.

"What was it about?" she asked, softly, and put her head on my chest.

"I guess… I don't know, you were asking what was on my mind, what was bothering me, and I was thinking about these time slips, but wasn't ready to tell you, and you got really upset, wanted to know what was I keeping from you, and …"

"I'm not angry now," she said, and rubbed my belly.

I put my hand over hers. This was unbelievable. She was unbelievable. The more I talked about these crazy time slips, the more she wanted to make love. And then it occurred to me – maybe she was turned on somehow by the time-slip talk. Maybe the idea of sleeping with someone who transgressed time was arousing to her.

I should be so lucky – but here she was, in my arms, and acting like she would love a third go. In the previous reality, we had argued bitterly because I hadn't told her what was on my mind. Now that I told her in this reality, we were having at it like Energizer bunnies. Maybe she was a secret fan of time travel. I'd been planning on asking her if she'd seen any of *Travelers*, with the new season about to start on Netflix –

She was rubbing my belly harder and lower and we did it again. And we got hungry. "Should we go out for dinner?" she asked. "I've got next to nothing in the fridge."

"Sure," I said. We both dressed. I went to the refrigerator anyway, and guzzled down a bottle of Poland Spring.

"We'll need an umbrella," Vanessa said, with a bright smile. "It's raining pretty hard outside."

"Right." We walked down the stairs, out into the street, and hunkered down under the big purple umbrella in the pouring rain. There was a good Italian restaurant just a few blocks away.

There were puddles on the sidewalk. We did our best to sidestep them. At one point, I stepped on a soggy newspaper some slob had left on the street and nearly lost my footing – probably the same paper I had stepped on in the rain in my prior reality.

"Be careful," Vanessa said and laughed. She clung more closely to my arm, as much to steady me as her. "If you slip back in time, we lose this whole afternoon, right?"

"Yeah, probably," I said, "unless I slip back just a few minutes."

"Well, let's not take any chances," she said, and wrapped herself around my arm. "I love you just the way you are right now."

We crossed the street. A car came too close and splashed us before we jumped out of the way.

"On the other hand," Vanessa said, "what do you think would happen if you slipped while I was holding on to you, and I fell down, too? Do you think we would both slip back in time, at the same time, together?"

"I don't know," I said, "probably not – for either of us – the slips so far had to be accidental to have that result. Nothing happens other than a bruised knee and ego if I deliberately fall down."

She nodded and held on to me tightly.

I kissed her forehead.

We stepped onto the sidewalk, and with all the rain and talk, we missed the broken curb –

THE LAST TRAIN TO MARGARETVILLE

First published in Walk the Fire 2, *edited by John Mierau, 2014.*

Margaretville is a good 2 and ½ hour car ride from New York City. A train would no doubt have been a little faster, but the last train to Margaretville arrived in 1942. Now, all these years later, in the second decade of the 21st century, the only way to get in and out of Margaretville was still just by bus or car. Well, that, and walking, if you weren't going too far.

And there's also that spot in the forest.

I was not too far from it now, sitting on a hill as a soft rain made dimples on the lake below. It wasn't strong enough to do the job. I needed to swim in the lake in an all-out pouring rain before I could proceed to the forest. "To wash yourself clean," she had told me. Like that old Fleetwood Mac song, right?

Margaretville had still not fully recovered from the floods caused by the hurricane three years ago in 2011. Those raging brooks had come down from the mountains and washed many a campsite, many a house, not just clean but clean away. But not the spot in the forest, which apparently had been able to take care of itself.

I walked back slowly to the house as the sun set. I had purchased it just a year ago from a New Jersey dentist who had summered here. He in turn had purchased the house from a farmer, whose father had built the house back in the 1930s.

I learned about the spot in the forest from an old surveyor's map — hand drawn, dated 1932, apparently made just prior to the house being built. There was a little square on the map marked "house" — likely where a previous structure had stood, and where the current house resided. The lake was clearly marked, as were the tree lines.

And well beyond one of those lines, at very edge of the survey map, was a strange sign, an amalgam of tiny angles upon angles.

It was from a language or culture unknown to me, and just cried out for investigation. I never found out if the dentist had known about it — he had moved with no forwarding address from his place in New Jersey. Even in this digital day and age, there was no record of him anywhere.

I showered and contemplated the lake trout I would grill for dinner. I had pulled it out of the lake just a few hours earlier. It was a lot to eat, but I was hungry. I turned my shower to ice cold — that was the way I liked to end my showers — stepped out, dried myself with an oversized towel, and dressed quickly in jeans and t-shirt. There was a sharp knock at the door.

She was standing outside. She had warned me, the first time we met, that she didn't believe in calling or texting. I doubted she even carried a phone. I opened the door and invited her in.

"Join me for dinner?" I asked her. There would be just enough trout to go around.

***

I got Glenn Miller's Moonlight Serenade on the iPhone playing in the background. Thinking about that last train in 1942 had put me in the mood for it. Glenn Miller must have been playing out of every radio in America back then.

My visitor seemed oblivious to the music. She did enjoy the trout. "They keep the lake well stocked," she said, and smacked her lips in approval.

I knew it was a waste of time to ask her who the "they" was. I knew I had never put as much as a leaf of duckweed into the lake myself. "It's supposed to be raining cats and dogs tomorrow," I said, thinking about the lake and its hard rain requirement. I refilled her glass with Pinot Grigio, as well as mine.

She nodded and sipped. "That's certainly the forecast. But

there are no guarantees."

I frowned.

"You bounders are always impatient," she said. "You can travel faster than just about anyone on this planet, but you're always moaning about delays."

"I only have your word for it that I'm a bounder," I shot back, "and impatience is a universally human quality." The bounder appellation, she had told me, came from rebound, or the ability she said I possessed to make a round-trip in the blink of an eye.

"You better hope I'm right," she said. "Your plan and your safety depend upon it. But ... if you're really the illustrator you say you are," she pointed to some of my work on the walls, "then there's no doubt you have the gift. The way you capture the journey of light through the world speaks to your synchrony with the flame." She looked for an extra moment at a grouping of pen-and-ink drawings of boats, trains, and planes — one of my specialties.

It was always nice to be appreciated. "You're quite the art critic, for just a real estate agent," was all I said. But I knew she was far more than that, and the real estate business was just a convenient cover. I regarded her. Something about her face made me feel I was looking at her for the first time, every time I looked at her. She was in her mid-30s, had long auburn hair, slightly almond eyes, and was reasonably attractive. Ordinarily, I would have thought about asking her to stay the night, or at least a few hours. Hey, I was divorced. But I had more important fish to fry. I speared the last of my tender trout with my fork.

***

I once again considered my options after she left.

I had the need, no doubt. She liked my illustrations — this Lanterna, as she had asked me to call her — but not everyone else in the world agreed with her. The recession had hit me hard. All five of my corporate contracts had been cancelled, and my deal with the US Mint put on hold. But my alimony for a wife and daughter she barely let me see — that of course continued unabated. And this house wasn't exactly given to me at a discount either. I'd paid top dollar for this house by the lake, with a disadvantageous mortgage, right before my corporate cancellations began rolling in. I needed money, and no bank was likely to give a starving artist a loan.

Desperate needs breed desperate measures. I had an idea of how to get my hands on some tidy sums. The question was how to keep them, and not end up in prison for all of my efforts.

By the way, I'm not perfect, but I'm a fundamentally honest man. I would never steal from an innocent person. My plan was to recoup money owed to me by deadbeats — three of them, to be exact, who had put my work to good use, and then neglected to pay me. They were all far wealthier than I could ever be, and lawyered to the hilt. It would take me years in court before I had a chance to present my story to a judge or jury. At least, that's what my own lawyers had told me — both of them. I had left the first because I didn't like his advice, and the second had said exactly the same.

Good thing I had run into Lanterna by the spot in the forest. My guess is she had the place wired up in some way to give her a signal any time anyone came near it. Not that you could tell by looking at it — just old rock, the kind they used to make those old stone walls with, and a strange glow emanating from within. It caught my eye immediately. I had asked her if she somehow had a video camera or whatever pointed at this place, and she never answered. She seemed to only say what she wanted to say, regardless of questions put to her.

I had no idea if she knew the purpose of my planned trips to New York. She never asked and I never told her. If anything she seemed encouraging, despite all of her attitude. It felt as if she wanted me to go.

Breaking into those three homes would not be a problem — that was easy enough. My uncle had been a safecracker in his spare time, back in the day, and he taught me some things. No, the key was having an airtight alibi. Like being in the Binnekill Restaurant off Main Street in Margaretville at more or less the same time as the break-in in New York. More than a two-hour drive from here to there. No way anyone could be in those two places at almost the same time. Unless he had access to that spot in the forest with what Lanterna called the flame.

***

The sun was bright the next morning, just what I didn't want to see.

I walked the property and tried to enjoy it as best I could. The wildflowers were especially beautiful. Soon there would be orange salamanders walking delicately on the ground around the flowers. They were my favorite.

The plan for my three jaunts was to have a nice dinner at the Binnekill — their schnitzel was delicious — talk it up with the waitresses, make a memorable impression of my patronage, and then head back to the house and that spot in the forest.

First I had to make a test run — both to satisfy myself that this flame really worked, and to set in motion my creation of some crucial ID.

But before I could do that, I had to swim in this lake in the pouring rain, and the sun just wasn't cooperating. It continued high and shining in the sky through the day.

I walked back to the house to fetch some sketching materials. This was a pretty good second best to traveling to New York instantly. Nah, it didn't hold a candle to that, but I did so enjoy it. I started sketching a train ...

I was awoken by a big grumbling clap of thunder. I looked at my sketch. It was about half finished. I'd dozed off. I looked at the clock on the wall. It was 6:15 in the evening. The sky clapped again, like a crack on the rim of a drum, this time followed by a growing pitter-patter brush stroke of ... rain!

I looked outside. It was really coming down. I hastily stripped, ran out of the house and into the lake. The property was secluded so there was little chance of anyone seeing me, and, besides, I didn't want to risk this being just a momentary downpour and lose my opportunity in the time it took to get on a bathing suit. Rainstorms started and ended that quickly here in the mountains.

The water felt cold and good and cleansing indeed. I swam

several minutes, head drenched by rain, the rest of my body under water, and then back to shore.

I dressed quickly back at the house. I left my iPhone on the table. That was the one thing that really unsettled me about this whole business — I felt naked proceeding anywhere without my phone. This was an odd world we live in. Or maybe I was the one who was odd. I don't have qualms about swimming naked in a lake, I'm not overly perturbed about walking through a flame and arriving instantly in New York City, but I'm discomforted going anywhere without my phone. But I didn't have a choice in this case.

The last thing I needed was some NSA or whatever data tracking organization having evidence from the GPS in my phone that I had been in two places at almost the same time. I did take the big wad of cash I had put aside for this occasion, and some non-digital old-fashioned IDs from my wallet.

I proceeded to the spot in the forest.

***

It was a 15-minute careful walk through a dense forest, mostly of pine and maple, and an intense underbrush that could trip you up if you weren't careful. It was highly unlikely that anyone would stumble on the spot — I of course had arrived here the first time guided by the surveyor's map.

The sun was a few minutes from setting when I reached the spot. The glow from the inside of the structure was soft and gently flickering, the kind of light a bulb on the ceiling might make if there was a fan slowly spinning below it. But this light came from a flame in an old stone fireplace on the ground — a single, wide flame about 10 feet high.

I knew about the heat. I had been here before. Lanterna had assured me that once I got closer to it, about to walk into it, all would be cool — and then I would be transported. Up until now, I had been glad that Lanterna had told me she would not be here, because I didn't need her that much into my business. But now I suddenly felt otherwise. I breathed in deeply. This was not a time to panic. If I proceeded into the flame and felt at all singed, I could quickly withdraw. I wouldn't just stand there like a bride in some traditions and allow myself to get burned to death by the flame.

I walked to the flame. I felt the heat and involuntarily shut my eyes, but then I opened them and squinted. I wanted to see what was happening. And it suddenly felt cool. I opened my eyes wide and saw colors changing to shades of every possible tomato — red, orange, yellow, everything in between. I took one step further and found myself in what looked and smelled like a dank basement.

***

I gave my eyes and myself a few seconds to adjust to the new surroundings. I was in a dimly lit room of some sort, no longer in the forest. But was it the tunnel under Fordham University in the Bronx?

Lanterna had given me a paper map, which I had memorized and carried in my pocket for back-up. I had grown up in the neighbourhood, on the other side of White Plains Road. I had also extensively researched the place, and all of this coincided with what I had seen of Fordham the few times I had guest-lectured in art classes over the years. Keating Hall was constructed in the 1930s on Fordham University's Rose Hill campus in the Bronx — about 30 minutes by train from the first home I intended to burglarize, in Yonkers. I wouldn't have minded a closer point of entry, but beggars — or bounders, to use Lanterna's term — couldn't be choosers.

Tunnels beneath Keating definitely existed. I looked at the multi-hued shimmering flame that was now a few steps behind me. The question was where exactly were it and I in the Keating tunnel system — assuming I indeed was now in the tunnels under Keating.

I hoped I was not too far from the University Bookstore above as indicated on the map. It called for me to walk about 15 feet, open a door, climb a staircase, walk several hundred feet, climb another set of stairs, open a door and that would bring me to a lower level of Keating which snaked and turned and eventually brought me near WFUV, Fordham's radio station.

Good thing I had brought my powerful little LED flashlight with me — I had almost left it in Margaretville, because I was so accustomed to using the flashlight app on my phone, which I had left at home. I didn't see light in the tunnels until I reached the level with the radio station. And I didn't know I was at Fordham University for sure until I saw the FUV offices. I sauntered by, so as not to attract attention, but I had all I could do not to jump in the air and shout "Yes!!" This insane flame thing had actually worked for me!

The University Bookstore was right across the street from Keating Hall. I had checked on its hours — it was open until 9pm on this summer evening, because summer school was still in session. I walked into the bookstore — it was empty of customers, not a good thing — but I quickly saw what I needed. I picked up the cheapest camera with Internet connections, brought it to the cashier — a redhead with freckles and white pants that looked like they'd been spray painted on — and made my purchase. I slipped in the batteries, made sure the camera and its Internet connection worked, and walked a suitable distance away from the counter.

Now came the hard part. I had to wait for some guy, any guy, to make a purchase, and hope that he displayed a university ID card to get a student or faculty discount. But how long could I wait without looking suspicious? I walked a few steps further away from the counter and pretended to carefully read the start-up instructions on my camera, though I knew exactly how it worked.

Some five minutes later, a guy in his twenties, likely a student, entered the bookstore. He picked up a gym bag — they were on sale — and approached the counter. He pulled out his wallet and paid with cash. Great, no help at all.

I ambled even further away and pretended to be engrossed in some books required for a chem class. Three more customers came in, and not a single one showed a university ID card. I'd been here more than 15 minutes already. I had to wait as long as was necessary.

Fortunately, the redhead seemed oblivious to me, devoting every ounce of her attention when she wasn't ringing up a sale to her smartphone and some messaging that was making her smile, frown, and pout in slow procession.

A man entered the bookstore. I walked a little closer to the cashier so I could get a picture if an ID card was displayed. The man noticed me, and gestured that I should go first. I smiled graciously and muttered "after you." He proceeded to the cashier, picked up an oversized sweatshirt that was on sale, and gave it to the cashier.

"Do you have a Fordham ID?" she asked, sweetly.

"Absolutely," the man replied, and produced his ID.

Yes!

"Thank you, Professor Pilant," the redhead said, "this gives you a 25% discount." She gave the ID back to him.

And I left the bookstore. I had what I needed. Four photos of the professor's ID, which I looked at in the cool moonlight on the street outside of the bookstore. I uploaded the photos to Google Drive, Dropbox, and two other sites, just to be sure. I walked to Keating, and dropped the camera in a trash receptacle. When I got back to Margaretville, I'd access those photos, doctor them up, and use them to make a Fordham faculty ID for myself. Next time I traveled back here, I'd be able to leave the campus, pay a visit to the deadbeat's house in Yonkers, and come right back to this campus with no security guard questioning what I was doing here after I displayed my new ID.

***

The trip back to the house in Margaretville was a piece of cake. So was accessing the photos I had uploaded at Fordham, and then producing a Fordham ID with my photo and Pilant's name. I also produced an ID with my photo and my name, and my photo and a bogus name. Depending on who asked to see it, I'd make a decision about which one to present. With any luck, the security guard would not know what Professor Pilant looked like. Fordham University was a big school.

I was ready to go the next morning. Unfortunately the weather was not. I suffered through six sunny days. I was like a damn farmer already, praying for rain. I cursed and railed against the good weather, and tried to console myself with the thought that even miracles come with strings attached.

I consoled myself further with the greatest continuing consolation in my life, my drawings. I finished the last train to Margaretville — that's what that drawing had become — and began to sketch something else. Then I put that aside and started a watercolor. It was something I'd never attempted before — the soft, blurry shades of a dozen tomatoes, each a slightly different color—

And I looked outside and saw it was beginning to rain. I almost hated to be pulled away from my painting, but the rain took precedence. I took off my clothes and waded into the lake. It was raining hard now.

The bathing would be good for me to go through the flame for 24 hours, Lanterna had told me. It was now about 3 in the afternoon. My next stop would be the Binnekill Restaurant for dinner at 6pm.

***

Jaeger schnitzel — hunter's schnitzel, not breaded, just veal in a mushroom sauce — has long been one of my favorite dishes. I'd ordered it the two previous times I'd been in the Binnekill in the past year, and it had been mouth-watering both times.

"Good to see you again," the hostess who was also a waitress greeted me with a smile, "haven't seen you here in a while." She was blonde, long neck, long hair, in her early 30s, and I thought what I always think when I see a woman like that. I'd like to paint her in the nude — tell her I was using her as a model for a Greek goddess — and go on to do more. But tonight I had even more pressing matters on the table.

"Yeah, I've been busy with my illustrations," I said, and ordered the Jaeger schnitzel.

"Are you an artist? I didn't know that," she said, and smiled at me again.

So far, this was going exactly as if my goal were indeed to paint and bed her.

"What kind of things do you paint?" she asked me.

"Nature, in all its forms," I replied. "And I also have an eye for transportation technology." At this point, I sometimes threw in a joke about having an affinity for cabooses, but I refrained this time.

"You have a good place for the nature up here," she said. "Is your work on display anywhere?"

"Just in a few galleries here and there," I said. "I'm building up my catalogue."

She nodded and left to place my order. She returned with it about 10 minutes later.

"Jaeger schnitzel," she said, and placed the dish on my table with a flourish. "Can I get you anything else? A little beer with your schnitzel?"

If only I didn't have plans for this evening. But I had only my fantasies that she would be willing to pose for me, and it likely wouldn't have happened this evening in any case.

"No, I'm fine," I replied. I needed a clear head for the rest of the evening. I figured this conversation would be more than enough for her to remember me if anyone thought I was in New York just minutes from now.

"You know, my husband is an art dealer," she said.

"Really? You're kidding!"

"No, it's true," she said. "And I'd be happy to tell him about your work. Do you have a card?"

"I certainly do," I said and reached into my pocket. We exchanged cards. Funny how this world works — just when I was about to steal someone's money to pay my bills, a possible source of income pops up unexpectedly at a restaurant. But whatever her husband could do for me, it would likely provide a pittance of the money in hand I would be getting in New York tonight before the end of the hour.

I finished my schnitzel quickly, declined dessert, and left a 50% tip. She would 100% remember me.

***

The walk to the spot in the forest was no problem, as was the walk through the tunnels of Keating and my exit from the campus. No one asked for my ID — no one cares who are you when you're leaving.

I caught the Metro North at the Fordham Road station and took it down to 125th Street. I switched to the uptown Harlem line to Ludlow. I had all of this timed to under 30 minutes. A cab would have been a little faster, but I didn't need a cabbie complicating matters as a witness to my being here.

I exited the station and walked uphill to the deadbeat's house. I had picked this guy first because his house would be the easiest. It was in Yonkers, the closest to Fordham. I knew where he kept his stash of cash — in a drawer in his bedroom, which I had seen through an open door the one time I had previously been in the house and he paid me. And I knew the layout of the house outside and the rock under which he kept his extra key.

I had been hired to thoroughly sketch the house when the deadbeat thought he was putting it up for sale, and had come upon the key when I had moved a few rocks to getter a better vantage point for one of the sketches. And I also knew that he and his family were currently in Maine in a summer house.

Still, I had to be very careful. The last thing I needed was a nosy neighbor calling the cops. They wouldn't be impressed at all with my Fordham ID.

Fortunately, the house was unattached. I walked around to the side which had the rock. I had to do this quickly. Every minute that I stayed here increased the possibility of someone noticing there was someone in the house.

The key was in a plastic bag where it should have been. I took it out, walked to the side entrance, and unlocked the door. No alarms that I could hear went off. I was in!

I walked to the bedroom, opened the drawer, and helped myself to the hundred-dollar bills in several envelopes. I took as many envelopes as the deep pockets in my pants and jacket could carry. I figured I had seven or eight thousand dollars here. That should help pay some bills. It certainly covered the money the deadbeat owed me, and a little more for my troubles.

I walked quickly back to the door, and spotted another bunch of envelopes in an open drawer. I had room for a few more. I took one of the envelopes. It didn't feel like it had money. It was filled with medical bills—

A car drove by — I could see the lights outside. I froze.

Fortunately the car kept moving. I resumed breathing.

I read through the medical bills quickly. The deadbeat's boy had a serious heart condition that required repeated surgery. Repeated surgery that was very expensive. Didn't this guy's family qualify under Obamacare? I couldn't tell. The deadbeat was a self-employed contractor. He clearly cut corners with everything, and apparently not only with the money he owed me but in getting decent health insurance. The heart surgeries for his son were draining him dry.

His boy needed heart surgery. But my heart, though often muddled, was I guess in the right place when it came to this deadbeat. I couldn't take thousands of dollars of his money and leave his son to the wolves of uncertain medical care. I cursed loudly, was glad there was no nearby neighbour to hear it, and returned the envelopes with the money to the bedroom drawer.

I left the house and walked quickly down to the Ludlow station to take the trains back to Fordham. Of all the rotten luck — but I'd just have to do better with the next deadbeat. I briefly considered whether I should continue on the train to Grand Central, and pay a visit to the second deadbeat's place, which was in a ritzy high-rise in lower Manhattan. Tempting— but no, I needed to vet that plan. It was dangerous just tacking it on to what I was doing tonight.

I was back outside the Fordham campus 26 minutes later.

***

I approached the security guard and casually waved my ID — the one with my picture and Pilant's name. The guard didn't even look at it. I could have had a picture of George Washington on the card.

***

The flame in the tunnel way under Keating Hall looked especially beautiful tonight. I'd never seen such a spectrum of light. And so did the flame in the forest in Margaretville — a mirror image of the Keating Hall beauty, which made it just as beautiful itself.

I ran into a string of sunny days. Even the wildflowers looked parched. I busied myself with my watercolors. I had several of them now. My phone rang one day in the late afternoon. The number looked slightly familiar. It was the husband of the blonde in the Binnekill. He wanted to look at my work, and was wondering if he could come right over. "Sure," I told him, and gave him directions.

He pulled up in a Mini Cooper about 15 minutes later. Give him credit not only for a nice-looking wife but a nice looking car. He shook my hand, and then took a careful look at all of the drawings hanging on my wall. He started to say something, then noticed the three watercolors on my table. I had not yet put them on the wall.

"What are these?" he asked. "They're really striking."

"Just a study in shades of red, orange, and yellow," I replied. No point in telling him about the flames.

His eyes dilated, I hoped with the pleasure of looking at the watercolors. "There's something more in those images - an intensity, an inner life in the flames, that I've never seen before. I may have a buyer for these. Are you interested?"

I shook my head yes and we discussed terms. I quoted prices in the thousands of dollars, far more than I was accustomed to getting for my work.

He nodded, said he be in touch, and left.

He came back the next day and paid me my price for all three of the watercolors. It started to rain after he left, and heavily, but I barely noticed. I was too busy painting.

***

I sold 10 paintings to him over the next few weeks. He paid cash for all of them. I paid all of my bills, got up to date in my alimony, and even bought my daughter a birthday present that was close to her heart — front row tickets to a Thom Yorke concert.

"Is this all the same buyer or a group of people?" I asked the dealer, as he left with the eleventh and twelfth of my efforts.

"I really can't tell you," he replied, softly. "You understand."

I guess I did. Dealers had to keep the buyers out of contact with the painters, otherwise the painters could deal with the buyers directly.

But I needed to know. Who was this wealthy buyer who was saving my life?

I came up with a plan. I began including faint outlines of people in my watercolors of the flames. I put in one face in particular.

And sure enough, there's was a knock of my door one evening, three days after I'd sold the watercolors with the flames and the faces.

Lanterna entered and smiled at me. "I see you haven't taken advantage of the nasty weather we've been having," she said.

"No, otherwise occupied," I replied. "I just knew you were the buyer," I told her, and she sat at the table and regarded a watercolor I had just finished, which had her face.

"A logical deduction," she replied.

"And ... you're not angry that I'm doing this?" I said, "getting word out to the world, or images out to the world, of the flames?"

"Well, as long as I keep buying them, you're only getting word out to me," Lanterna said. "And not the world, not just yet. The flames and what they do are secret."

"Wouldn't it be easier to kill me?" I half joked.

"Certainly cheaper," she replied. "But we're not murderers."

"Good to know," I said.

"And besides," she continued, "your watercolors provide a record of the flames very precious to me and my kind. The flames evade portrayal by chemical or digital photography. They just look like, well, conventional, unremarkable flames when photographed. Your talent captures something of their true beauty and power."

"Thank you," I said, genuinely touched by her words. "Would you care for some wine, a bite to eat?" I was in a celebratory mood.

"I think I would," Lanterna said and smiled.

I gestured for her to sit at the table.

"How did you know I could walk from here to New York

through the flame?" I asked her.

Lanterna smiled. "I saw some of your work in town. I could see that you had a special kind of eye for light ... people with such vision have a high likelihood of being sensitive to the flames, to be able to jaunt home and back or sometimes even farther.
But I have a confession to make - what I told you about needing to be cleansed was a bit of fib. I wanted to slow you down a bit, give you time to think. And when you started painting them, what wonders you captured. Waiting for the rain was the perfect prescription."

I went to get the wine, and looked at the last illustration I had put on the wall. The last train to Margaretville. It would be the last train to Margaretville or anywhere I'd be drawing for a long time. From now on the only mode of transport I would be painting were those glorious flames.

IAN, GEORGE, AND GEORGE

First published in Analog, *December 2013.*

I an walked towards his little shop on Johnson Avenue in the Bronx, looked up at the glowing neon sign that proclaimed its name, and scowled. He had programmed the neon to flicker, just a little, last week. To give it a touch of mid-20th century authenticity, a time that was especially appealing to him because it was just beyond the range of his agency. But now that he looked at the cool neon script, flickering in a pattern designed to look random, he was concerned that customers might not get the historical detail, and mistake the effect for a faulty sign. That was unacceptable — the last thing Ian wanted to do was introduce any uncertainty into the minds of customers who were paying him a lot of money for a trip to the past and back. An unstable sign, after all, could also be a sign of an unstable system that provided shoddy access to a vent in the space-time continuum.

I looked at Ian shaking his head on the screen in my hand from my vantage point around the corner. I smiled. If I knew Ian, he was thinking about whom could he blame for this blunder in self-proclamation. And I knew Ian a bit about now. I'd made it my business to know everything I could about this consummate businessman, including installation of a variety of micro-cameras to record his moves near and in his store, which I was reasonably sure he didn't know about. It was the least I could do, given that I was about to put a lot of money — not to mention my life — in his hands, once again.

Ian entered the building. I gave him a few minutes to get up to his "Ian's, Ions, and Eons" on the second floor, and I walked over to conduct our business.

***

He was still scowling when I entered his office — presumably not about the sign, because it was no longer flickering when I reached the storefront. He looked up from behind the counter and nodded.

"All set?" I asked.

"I have your money and your signature," Ian replied, "all that I need." He looked at my papyrus-weave jacket. "I wouldn't wear that tomorrow — you'll be traveling into a brutal heat wave. Mid-90s Fahrenheit."

"Ok."

Ian reached under the counter and came up with a dark paisley vest. He rubbed the fabric between his fingers, as if he was fathoming the texture, and gave the garment to me. "I put nasal suppositories in the right pocket. You may need them, given the heat where you're headed, and the consequent smell."

"Thank you," I said. "But I like to savor everything in the places I visit, including the aromas."

"Suit yourself."

"I only wish there was some way I could go back a few decades further," I said. Not really, I was just saying that to gauge his reaction.

Ian's scowl deepened. "You know the limitations."

"I guess I'm thinking that limits are only absolute to the extent that someone has yet to figure out how to break through them."

Now Ian smiled, with scarcely more joy than conveyed in his scowl. "I don't care what you do or try to do about those limitations, as long as you're back on that northbound Metroliner on July 28, 1970."

***

It certainly wasn't too hot the next morning, as I walked up to Moynihan Station, gleaming in the sunlight on 33rd Street and

8th Avenue. In fact it was beautiful, and the air was sweet with the locust and hibiscus trees planted up and down the streets and along the new overpass, too. I breathed in slowly and sighed. A parting, living postcard, to wish me well and encourage my return.

I sauntered down the stairs. Plenty of time to catch the train. I bought a cool lemon-cantaloupe juice — my favorite for this early in the morning — and looked around. I wondered if I could spot Ian's train agent. There was a 66.66% chance her name started with "I," and a 33.33% chance it started with "E," but I didn't see nametags shimmering on anyone.

I leaned against a pillar and contemplated the holographic display on the far wall. Half a dozen Tricelas were approaching Moynihan from north and south, dicing up the light as they plied their ways through the morning. They were the closest emissaries of Biden North American InterRail, which glistened in the background on the screen like a great circulatory system made of phosphor. These would be the last three-dimensional images I'd be seeing for a while. Where I was going, it would all be two-dimensional, and inside rather than outside the screens.

***

I found my reserved seat on the train and tried to get comfortable. She soon took the seat next to me, in a snug, thin lavender outfit of linen.

"Iris," she said, and extended a hand.

I took it and started to tell her mine—

"No need for pleasantries," she said. "As you know, I'm just going to brief you here — briefly brief you," she smiled at her own wordplay, "and leave before the train pulls out."

"Right," I said. No pleasantries, but I couldn't help notice that she was aptly named, with rich earthy brown irises that warmed your soul.

"You've utilized Ian's twice before, with good results, so you know how this works — you make your move between Philadelphia and Wilmington."

"Yes," I said.

"This trip is a little more ambitious, but the fundamentals are the same. Ok ... any questions?"

"What happens if someone sees me in the Cafe Car, just as I'm —"

She waved a dismissive hand. "Not the problem that amateurs imagine it to be — as you know, because you're no amateur."

"I know," I said, "but I have still have concerns."

She waved her hand again. "Your disappearing would be chalked up as hallucination, if anyone happens to see it. You were wise to take the no-accompaniment option — you shaved some bucks off a very expensive trip, given that 1970 is so close to the terminus." She stood and smiled again. "I better get out of here before the train starts."

I watched her walk away down the aisle. I was known here as a generous patron of the arts, but sometimes I was too cheap for my own good. I wouldn't have minded Iris' company on the swift trip to Philadelphia.

***

The Cafe Car was crowded, which was probably, ironically, the best way to do this. Someone suddenly vanishing was a lot more likely to be noticed when one of a few, not a bustling many. I looked at my wristwatch, which I had already donned. One minute 18 seconds until the cosmos touched my shoulder and spun me like a top back to 1970, at the same exact time and day of the month as now. I stroked my paisley vest with my thumb. I hoped Ian had gotten the nano-weave right, which would pull me into the speed and angle and place of this train in the space-time fabric at the right moment and leave me in the same place on a very different train, a Metroliner, headed to Wilmington, Delaware in 1970. For some reason, I always worried about that weave the most, but it had worked as advertised twice before — actually, four times, traveling and returning, safe and sound, on two trips.

I receded into a corner, and tried to make myself as small and inconspicuous as possible. I stole a look at my watch. Just seconds to go now. I closed my eyes and—

***

That feeling never got old. I was smiling. That smell of beer — I didn't even drink the stuff anymore — but its smell was insistent, all around me, and told me before I opened my eyes a split second later that I was back in the past. Yeah, they liked their beer back here, and it had a more pungent smell than where and when I'd just been, and now the shirts and the jeans and the wide ties and moustaches and beads confirmed that I was in 1970 or some time pretty close to it. It was also sweltering in this car — beer, sweat, and an overlay of primitive air conditioning. I felt as if I was inside a big malfunctioning refrigerator with its doors flung open—

"George?" A redhead approached, and ushered me to the door. "The passenger cars are a little cooler," she said.

"You work for Ian?" I asked, but I knew she did.

"Yes, I'm Ilana." She held the door open for me. We walked to the next car, which was definitely less oppressive. She leaned again a seat. "No point in sitting, you'll be getting off in Wilmington in just a few minutes."

I nodded, and noticed her tight blue bell-bottom jeans. Perfect attire for near the end of the psychedelic era.

She gave me a small stuffed envelope. "You've got a round-trip ticket, Wilmington to New York today, New York to Wilmington tomorrow, and another ticket from Wilmington back to New York. Plus $500 in time-current cash."

"Thanks," I said.

She regarded me. "You don't mind traveling down here to Wilmington just to go back to New York?"

"Small inconvenience for a miracle," I said.

"I like your attitude," she said and patted my arm. A toucher — I liked that in a woman. "Be safe," she continued. "You chose the non-accompany option up to New York. I'll see you on the way back."

That was my cue to head for the doors.

"Wilmington. Wilmington, Delaware," the conductor announced on a too-loud speaker that hurt my ears.

***

I walked out of the train on to the Wilmington platform and looked for the stairs. I'm a big man, not as young as I used to be. I didn't mind the long walk down but didn't relish the prospect of the long walk back up to catch the northbound Metroliner to New York. I wasn't thrilled about the rickety elevator, either, but it was preferable to the stairs.

First I had to change into more 1970s-appropriate clothes. Given the anything-goes attitudes of this era, my garb hadn't attracted any undue attention on the Metroliner south of Philadelphia to here. But I didn't want to push my luck for the longer stay in New York, and I certainly didn't want to be wearing this vest on that northbound train, which could yank me right out of 1970 and back to the time I had just left. All of this in addition to my other reason for needing these new clothes.

I located the locker, exhaled with relief when the combination worked — I'm always anxious about combination locks, too - and retrieved the little satchel. Off to the men's room. I was too focused on changing clothes to hold my nose at the ambiance. But I glanced at the cut of my jib in the corroded mirror and was satisfied.

Back to the locker, deposit my just-removed future clothes, and up to the northbound train. It was right on time, nineteen minutes later.

***

I often wondered if there were others like me, people who had spent so much time in two times that they felt they belonged to both. Ian's files were impregnable, distributed in incomprehensible pieces in so many systems around the world that only one person could put them together — Ian, who carried the script for how to do that in his head. My visual surveillance of Ian's premises had given me plenty of images of Ian's customers. None jumped out at me as denizens of two times, and I certainly couldn't question them without risking Ian's anger and likely refusal to do any further business with me, i.e., take my money.

I took a long, slow breath as the Metroliner made its way beneath the Hudson on the last link in its journey to New York

City. I couldn't help feeling pretty good to be back here. Maybe it was these 1970 duds I had on, but my skin felt as if it belonged in this time and place. I realized that I was shaking my head and frowning. Whom was I kidding? There was a far deeper reason that made me feel I belonged here — I had been born in the 20th century, for chrissakes, and had lived here most of my life.

"New York City, Pennsylvania Station," the conductor announced. "Last stop."

***

I caught a cab on 8th Avenue. "Yorkville Restaurant, East 86th Street," I told the cabbie. "Know where that is?"

"No, you tell me when we get to 86," the cabbie replied in some sort of thick Slavic accent. If I'd put that in a movie, I'd be laughed out of the production. Truth could be funnier than fiction.

The Yorkville had one of the best cups of coffee in the city in this era. I looked forward to its fragrance and taste, but I wouldn't have time for more than one. I hoped my meeting with the go-ahead guy went quickly.

I directed the cabbie to the Yorkville, paid and tipped him and walked into the restaurant. Its dim lighting and smoky coolness were a welcome relief from the outside. I looked around and— Jeez, that Ian was full of surprises. Though I realized, as I often did, that nothing should surprise me about Ian.

I walked over to the table and extended my hand. "Elmyr de Hory ... no, no, please sit, no need to stand on my behalf."

Elmyr nodded. He looked tired, apprehensive about my speaking out his name, but appreciative that he didn't have to stand.

"How long have you been working for Ian?" I asked and sat at his table. "A coffee please," I said more loudly than Elmyr's name, and gestured to the waitress.

Elmyr waved my question away. "A once-in-a-while thing. Can't discuss," he spoke in a thick Hungarian accent. "Let's just say I like the money, and the protection, as you would know better than most."

"Ah yes, the forgeries."

Elmyr held a bony finger to his lips. "I'd like not to discuss that, either. My sole purpose now with you is to give the final green light on your project here."

"Understood," I said. The waitress arrived with my coffee. She looked older than my deceased grandmother. "It's a rather self-contained mission," I continued, "as you know."

Elmyr nodded. "But with its own dangers, anyway."

I lifted the coffee to my face. It smelled as good as ever. I sipped. The owner of the Yorkville likely had a relationship with some genius of a coffee supplier. I sipped some more, and looked at Elmyr. He'd been regarding me.

"You look good," he said. "The black outfit and the trimmed beard suit you."

I smiled. "Dressed for the part."

"But you did put on a few pounds," he added.

"Always a battle," I replied.

Elmyr produced an envelope from his shabby jacket. "Ilana gave you the tickets and the money. This is your 1970 ID, in case you need it." He gave me the envelope. "Your counterpart's laid up with a sudden asthma attack, sleeping now under doctor's orders, and the phone connection is blocked. I assured him before the medication that his appearance was cancelled. You're all set."

"That easy?" I asked. "Not that I'm complaining."

"I'm not really comfortable talking to you in these circumstances," Elmyr said. "You know me too well." He managed an unhappy smile. "But we're two pros at this, you and I. No point in prolonging. You know what I'll say. 'Easy to slip in the asthma trigger in room service food.' I know what you'll say. 'Yeah, I'm a soft touch for anything to eat.' Any more questions?"

I shook my head no.

"Good, then, best luck." He cleared his throat, stood up, and shook my hand. He threw down a crumpled dollar for the coffee he'd been drinking.

I looked at my watch as Elmyr left the restaurant. Still time for another coffee and maybe a quick bite, actually. "Could you fill this up?" I called out to Methuselah's mother and held out my cup.

"And a menu, too, please."

***

I caught a cab to the Elysee Theater on West 58th Street. I was a little early, I knew it, but Manhattan traffic was treacherous in any age and I couldn't risk being late. I was shown to the Green Room, offered a coffee — which I refused, so as not to disrupt the taste of the Yorkville's brew, still on my tongue. But I accepted the proffered cigar. I was seated by a big, woefully fat TV screen. Another show — not the Cavett — was close to concluding. It was being taped, as would be mine for broadcast later in the evening. Always struck me as strange that an interview on a television show would be taped rather than broadcast live — wasn't the big deal about television that it could be broadcast live, unlike a motion picture? — but that was the least strange in what was about to happen, and I had worked so hard to set in motion.

I lit my cigar and puffed. I had memorized everything I had said the first time, like words in a play, because I simply couldn't fathom what, if anything, might ensue in the world if I said anything significantly different this time. The interview on the screen concluded. The talent girl shortly appeared in a mini-skirt that was just perfect and escorted me to the back of the studio. She whispered that I would go on stage as soon as Mr. Cavett finished his monologue. Her lips near my ear excited me, but I had to focus on what was just ahead.

Cavett introduced me in glowing terms. He described me as "unique". I suppressed a chortle. I heard *Citizen Kane* and *War of the Worlds*. He quoted Charlton Heston and Kenneth Tynan about me. "Will you welcome ... Orson Welles."

I walked out to a big round of sustained applause. I soaked it in, because I could never get enough. I shook Cavett's hand and couldn't help smiling. I bowed slightly to the audience. I didn't get appreciated like this in the future. My own fault for disguising my real identity in that age — to just about everyone except a few close friends and Ian — and going with my first name, George.

The interview went just as I recalled, had seen, and rehearsed in the mirror at least a dozen times. I said goodbye to Cavett and left the studio. Part one of this business had concluded. I was looking forward to watching this on YouTube — still what, more than a quarter century away? — and seeing if I could notice slight differences in tone and delivery between this and my original interview on the Cavett show. There would be slight differences despite my best efforts, I knew that, even though the words were the same. I was my future self, not an exact copy of who I was now, after all. But that was actually the point of this.

***

I took a cab to my hotel on Madison Avenue — a few blocks from where my counterpart was now sleeping it off at the Barclay Hotel — and settled in for the evening. I couldn't resist rewarding myself with a little room service, but just of the culinary kind. It arrived quickly. I sipped and munched, and considered my next moves.

Part two of this operation was now commencing. I — or a reasonable facsimile thereof — had to be on that southbound Metroliner by tomorrow afternoon, to avoid arousing Ian's attention. This meant I had less than 24 hours to convince my younger self to take that excursion.

I fell asleep sooner than expected, awoke early the next morning, and had a fine breakfast of poached eggs and fresh figs. I headed over to the Barclay. I had no trouble getting a replacement for a "lost key" to my counterpart's room — after all, I looked just like him, give or take a few pounds. It occurred to me that I wouldn't have to go through even this little pretense in my new adopted age — Ian's age — since my iris would have been all that I needed to enter my counterpart's room. He of course had the same iris. Well, I guess there were some things I could miss about that age.

As I left the elevator and approached his room, I played a minor fantasy in my head. If he had been in bed asleep with one of his/my women — there were at least four possibilities, if memory served — and I managed to remove him from the bed, take off my clothes, and snuggle right up to her, would she realize the difference when she awoke? Not likely, even if she sensed I weighed a tad more. She wouldn't let herself entertain the cognitive dissonance, to say the least, that being in bed with some other version of him — me — would cause her.

I entered my counterpart's room. He was in bed alone, alas, as I knew he'd be. He awoke almost immediately. "What the hell?" He looked at me, rubbed his eyes and sat up too fast in bed. He grabbed the side of his back. I could feel his pain.

"You think you're dreaming," I said, as soothingly as possible. "You're not, but there's no way I can convince you of that right now. So you can just assume you're dreaming, let's talk, and eventually you'll know that you're not dreaming."

"You could spill cold water on my head, and if I don't wake up —"

"Nah, you know better than that — wouldn't prove a thing, no more than Samuel Johnson's kicking the stone proved anything," I said. "The water and the stone could still be part of your or God's or who knows who else's dream."

He almost smiled, then recalled something unpleasant. "How'd I get here? I was — wait — the asthma attack! I was given a drug — you're likely just a reaction to that, like Marley's ghost was the product of Scrooge's upset stomach."

I laughed. "Marley's ghost was real in *A Christmas Carol*, not a figment of Scrooge's unsettled imagination."

My counterpart nodded slowly and looked confused.

"It's ok. Just keep thinking that you're dreaming me and this conversation now, as I said. The important thing is that we talk."

"I was supposed to be on the Cavett show last night," my counterpart said.

I took a seat, even though none had been offered. "Actually, you were — or, in actual fact, I was."

"So ...," my counterpart began. "Mind you, I'm not accepting that you're anything more than a dream, though, at this point, who knows if you're a bad or a good one. But why—"

"I had your asthma attack induced, made sure you were drugged, and went on the Cavett show in your stead."

Now he laughed. "You — I — have a good imagination. I'll give you that. But why—"

I interrupted his same phrase again. I wanted to get to the point of this as soon as possible. "I wanted to establish me — my version of you, with whatever subtle differences — to the world back here as easily and quickly and graphically as possible. What better way than me not you appearing on Cavett?"

"And forgive me — I'd rather not keep saying 'but why' again — but the purpose of your wanting to establish yourself in my place back here was?"

I could tell he was enjoying this, at least a little. I doubted he'd enjoy what I was about to say to him. It would turn this presumed dream into a bit of a nightmare. "You're going to drop dead of a heart attack in 15 years — in 1985. I won't — I've already been treated for the condition and cured of it."

Right, now he wasn't smiling at all. "And where exactly would that be?"

"Not where, man, when. In the future, well after this century."

He shook his head, muttered something about needing some food to clear it, and went for the room service menu.

"Could you order the same for me?" I asked, softly. "You can afford the price of two breakfasts." I'd already eaten, but I had a much deserved reputation as a gourmand. And I didn't feel I was mooching -- I was pretty sure I'd wind up paying the bill, when I took control of his funds back here, and he did the same with some of mine in the future.

**

Our food arrived not long after. I opened the door, gestured to where the tray should be placed, and tipped the waiter.

"Thank you, Mr. Welles," he said, brightly. He glanced and nodded without really looking at my counterpart, who had put on a bathrobe. The waiter left the room.

I chuckled at the way he had avoided looking directly at my counterpart. Must have been his bathrobe. Better waiters and bellhops never looked long at anyone not fully clothed. "If you think she's naked, just look at her eyes, never a bit below, that's how we conduct ourselves in this profession," I had once heard a Brit dispense this advice.

My counterpart sat resignedly at the table. "He clearly saw you. I guess that's a point in favor of you being real," he said in that trademarked basso-profundo voice of ours.

"True, but not conclusive," I replied. "You still could be dreaming all of this, including the room service delivery."

He nodded, took a piece of his egg over easy, and smacked his lips. "So you come from the future, back to Mr. Dickens and his ghosts, or my almost namesake, Wells, Herbert George," he said.

"That's right," I said, and took a bit of the egg myself. Delicious. "But the actual reality of time travel is far more complex than Dickens or even H. G. imagined."

"Of course," my counterpart said. "Reality is always crazier than fiction." He gestured to me. "Why don't you sketch out your whole story, as long as you're here in my dream or whatever. There could be a script in this, me thinks."

"I knew you'd warm up to this," I said. "Here's the nub of it: I'm a future version of you — or, you, in the future. I've been cured of what will cause a massive, fatal heart attack in you, as I indicated. I came back here, and am talking to you now, with the goal of getting you to return to the future in my stead, so you can receive our life-saving treatment."

"But ... hasn't that already happened? I mean ... if you are here now, and you are my future self as you claim to be, doesn't that mean that I already went into the future, and received that treatment?"

"You're good," I said, and nodded in appreciation of my earlier self's quick grasp of some of the issue. "But, as I told you, time travel in reality — at least insofar as I know it — is far more complicated than what H. G. Wells wrote about in *The Time Machine*."

"Enlighten me."

I took the pot of coffee, and poured some for myself and my counterpart. "I remember my being you. I recall this very conversation, except I was sitting in your seat, and I don't know who the hell was sitting in mine — well, I wasn't sure then, thought it was a dream, just as you do, now -- but now I, sipping this coffee and talking to you, of course do know it was me, back then, the future version of you that I am right now."

My counterpart shook his head slightly. "I'm thinking I may need something stronger than food and coffee. But yes, isn't what you just said tantamount to what I was just saying about this conversation — and I assume everything after — having already happened? But—"

"I don't really know how free will fits into this," I responded. "You believe you have control over your actions, right?"

"As much as any man," he chuckled and cleared his throat.

"Well, then, that's why I'm here to convince you to do this — to travel into the future in my stead. Because, I'd rather not contemplate what would happen if you did not."

"Try me," he requested.

"I'd likely blink out of existence, the instant you decided not to travel to the future," I replied, "which would confirm your sense that this is a dream. Or maybe I never would have showed up this morning — or last night, on Cavett — at all."

He sipped his coffee, very slowly. "Given that there is a good chance that this is just a dream — and one I'm now actually becoming quite fond of — and, if not, well, it would be exciting, astonishing, to see what the future is like, I think I can say I'm game to do this." He thrust his hand across the table, for me to shake.

I shook it. "Good, I'm relieved."

"So, how would this work? I just step outside the door to this room and into your future?"

"Not quite so simple," I replied.

***

We spent the rest of the morning and a good part of the afternoon discussing what was not quite so simple. Most of it was the plethora of detail he had to know about my future life in order to pass for me. And then there was Ian.

"He thinks it will be me returning to the future, not you," I said.

"You told me you paid a small fortune for this trip," my younger self replied. "Why the hell should he care?"

"Trust me, he cares," I replied. "I paid for a trip to sit in for you on Dick Cavett — I knew he wouldn't be likely to object to that. But that's a far cry, a universe of difference, from you returning to the future instead of me."

"So raise more funds and pay the man for the different mission."

I shook my head no. "Ian is not just about money, though he likes to give the impression that it's all he cares about. But he also has an abiding concern, an unclear but I suspect absolute list of do's and don't's, about what he allows his customers to do on their trips to the past."

"Who is this guy?"

"I've studied him. I've learned a lot, but he's still a cypher."

My counterpart shook his head and scoffed, slightly. "We're the same person — more alike than identical twins. Ian obviously knows you traveled to the past. He'll assume it's you who's returned. If he notices any difference in our affect, in my mien versus yours, he'd attribute that to the impact of this very trip on you, wouldn't he?"

"I suppose," I said. "Look, I'm not trying to talk you out of this — last thing I would do — I just want you to be as aware as possible of what you'll be up against when you give the vest back to Ian."

***

We swapped wallets, clothes, and I made sure my counterpart had my ticket for the 4:25pm southbound Metroliner from Penn Station. I continued to brief him, and we left in time to catch the train.

Leaving the hotel separately would have been a little less likely to attract attention, but I figured the greater risk still resided in his bolting when he left my sight, so we walked out of the hotel together. I hailed a taxi — less exposure than taking the subway, and less than walking from here to Penn Station, would which have been too tiring for us, anyway, especially in this torrid heat.

We might even get an air-conditioned cab — there were some of them already in service in 1970 — and if not we'd roll down the windows, and cool down the good old-fashioned way.

"You know, I met H. G. once, in a radio interview in Texas in 1940," my younger self mused, as our taxi slowly made its way with wide-open windows down Seventh Avenue.

"I know, I remember," I replied, and indeed recalled that with pleasure.

"Amazing man," my counterpart continued. "He even plugged *Citizen Kane* in that interview. After he thanked me for sparking more sales of *War of the Worlds*."

I nodded.

"Seems like a dream, another lifetime," he continued. "Was I dreaming that, too?"

"You're not dreaming this and you weren't dreaming that," I said.

"And the insane thing is, I think I almost believe you," he said.

I squeezed his shoulder. "I'm glad. You should."

"His name is George, too, as you know," my counterpart mused. "Herbert George Wells. So in addition to having the same last name except for one letter, we both share a same given name — George Orson Welles, Herbert George Wells ... Was he somehow us, too???"

I chuckled. "Not likely," I said. "His voice was much higher, and he had a great British accent."

"I suppose anything is possible in a dream, though," my counterpart said.

***

I realized that our cab hadn't moved much in the past few minutes. We were on 38th Street and Seventh Avenue — just a few minutes away from Penn Station — but only, of course, if our taxi was moving. I looked at my watch.

My counterpart saw that, and did the same with his. "We have 35 minutes to get to the station. Shouldn't be a problem, assuming—"

"Yeah." I hadn't wanted to get to the station too early —

so as not to attract attention as big twins, especially not Ilana's attention, if she happened to be somewhere in the waiting room. But missing the train was unacceptable.

Our cabbie honked his horn. Didn't do any good. I stuck my head out the window, craned my neck, and saw the problem: an overheated car about half way down the block, hood in the air, steaming like a hot dog stand. Traffic was frozen in the heat. Our cabbie honked again and turned his head around to us. "Sorry," he said. "Bad time of day."

I pulled out my wallet and paid him. "Keep the change."

My younger self and I got out of the taxi. "We'll have to walk it," I told him.

"Obviously," he said, grunted, and wiped his brow.

It was hotter outside than in the cab. Fortunately, we both were dressed for it. But I had to be careful not to make my counterpart walk too fast, given his health. If he dropped dead right here in the street, so would I — or disappear, at any rate.

I continued to go over details with him. We stopped for a few beats at every corner, so he could catch his breath. I appreciated the breaks, too.

We reached the station, with 16 minutes to spare. We were both sweating profusely. "You can wash up in the bathroom on the train," I told my counterpart. "They're not too bad in this era."

"I know," he said.

"Right." I described Ilana again. "You'll enjoy looking at her body."

That got a smile from him.

"Make sure you see a doctor as soon as you get home — to my home," I said. "You'll find listings on any screen. Get that heart taken care of, first order of business. There may be other things you'll need to do, later on — other trips through time. All in due course. I don't want to overload you now."

"Considerate of you," he half growled, laughed, then coughed — and suddenly grabbed his chest and winced in pain—

God no! I started to react—

He doubled over in pain.

I put my arms around him and tried to hold him up—

He broke free, staggered— and laughed heartily. "Sorry — only joking!"

Good, he was ok. "Thanks — that almost gave *me* a heart attack." I mock punched him in the arm, and kept an eye on him as he walked towards his train. I turned and went back out into the heat. A fine little piece of acting on his part. But of more interest to me now was that apparently the past could be changed, at least slightly. I was 99% sure I had not feigned that heart attack the first time around.

***

I took a taxi back to what was now my hotel room — unlike the taxi, blessedly air conditioned. I stretched out on the bed. The maid had tidied the room. I'd have to remember to give her a big tip. I wondered how long it would take before I got any indication that my younger self had made it back to the future ok. I didn't have to wait long. The phone in the room rang.

"Mr. Welles?" the receptionist at the front desk asked me. "A man by the name of 'Elmer' here to see you, with a friend."

I thought for a quick second. I supposed I could run from this now, but I was tired, and, besides, sooner or later I'd have to face it. "Thank you — please send them up."

They knocked on my door a few minutes later.

I opened it with a smile.

There stood Elmyr de Hory and the friend — Ian.

***

I invited them in. Elmyr cracked a craggy grin. Ian looked just as he had every time I'd seen him — a scowl etched on his face. But it was little disconcerting seeing him out of his element, away from his shop with the neon sign.

"So you recovered all right from the asthma?" Elymyr asked, now straight-faced.

For a split second, I thought maybe Elmyr — and therefore Ian — thought I was my younger self, whom Elmyr had inflicted with asthma yesterday, and I had just brought to Penn Station less than an hour ago. No, these guys were way too smart for that.

Elmyr smiled again. "Had you going for a minute there, didn't I? It was good seeing you at the Yorkville last night," he said, just so I'd know for sure that he knew for sure just who I was.

"Same here." Everyone was the comedian today. I gestured to a small table. The three of us pulled up chairs.

I looked at Ian, and recalled an old theater adage. There were some actors who found the spotlight, wherever they happened to be on stage. They stole the scene, were stars, whatever the script and the director might have intended. Ian, sitting here, had that talent.

He spoke right up. "You're in gross violation of the itinerary," he said to me.

"What can I do to compensate you?" I replied, knowing better than to deny his allegation.

"The pertinent clause says that if you don't return, I'm entitled to seize all of your assets."

I considered. "Someone with my DNA, my memories, even the nasal suppositories you left in my vest pocket, did return."

"True," Ian said. "But not all of your memories. Not you."

"True," I replied. "But you'd have a hard time proving that."

"He's younger than you," Ian said.

"Precise age isn't so easy to scientifically ascertain — the world wears our bodies in different ways."

Ian nodded his acknowledgement of the point.

"And would you really want to make a Federal — or whatever it would be — case of this?" I pressed my advantage.

"No, but given your considerable assets in my time, I would risk it," Ian said. "I could petition to have all the legal proceedings private, sealed from the public. I have friends in good places."

I had likely reached the limits of my argument.

Ian saw that I realized that.

"May I ask how you found out? And when?" I knew Ian could have realized the switch any time in the future, and, whenever that was, set his visit to today.

"He told me," Ian answered, matter-of-factly.

"He? You mean ... my younger self?"

"That's right, and he told me right away." Now I got that slight smile from Ian, worse than his scowl.

"Did he at least get his heart fixed?"

"Your heart's fine, isn't it?" Ian said. "I sent him straight to the doctor, as soon he told me your story."

I touched my chest, breathed in and out, and considered. "So take all of my damned money in the future — that'll bankrupt him, not me." And I had squirreled away a sizeable portion of my funds in the future, for whenever I returned. It was likely beyond Ian's and definitely my younger self's reach .... But was Ian telling me the truth about my younger self? I certainly had no recollection of having had such a conversation with Ian as my younger self. But he probably had panicked for some reason, this time around, when he finally became convinced that what was happening to him wasn't a dream, but—

"There may be another way," Ian said, "something you could do for me that would balance the books."

Here it came. As I had told my younger self, Ian had goals that went way beyond the money he always claimed he was all about .

***

I had breakfast in the Barclay the next morning — eggs over easy, English muffin, fresh figs, and orange juice, fresh squeezed. I had to admit — eggs didn't taste quite as good in the future.

My waiter, Lenny, was talkative. "Saw you on Cavett the other night — you were excellent. Can I offer a little casting advice?"

"Sure." I'd likely get it whether I agreed or not.

"You ought to cast Brando in your next movie — Brando! — he's still the best. And Bronson as supporting actor. You see the body on that guy? I wish I could be in such good shape."

"Tell me about it," I said, only a little less tartly than the orange juice.

Lenny laughed. "Hey, you're entitled. You're the director, for godsakes. Doesn't matter what you look like."

"I used to act. Still do, sometimes."

"Point taken," Lenny said, and clapped me on the back. "But can I give you a little more advice — in your capacity as director?"

"Sure."

"George Pal did a fine job with *War of the Worlds* and *Time Machine* –– I actually liked his *Destination Moon* and *When Worlds Collide* better — but you could a better job, really, with any H. G. Wells story."

I nodded. "Thank you."

"He sometimes stays here when he's in from Hollywood," Lenny said, quietly, conspiratorially. "Wouldn't say he's a pal of mine, but almost." Lenny laughed at his own pun. "Don't tell Mr. Pal I said anything about his movies. But I'm telling ya, you're the director as far as H. G. Wells goes."

***

I don't know if anyone else has ever had this experience, but I sometimes almost think that waiters are reading my mind — and not about food — when they recognize me and give me advice.

I left a generous tip on my room tab, patted off whatever may have been left of the egg on my face –– visible and otherwise, for the many failures and unfulfilled projects in my life. Well, this was one project I could not afford to leave hanging. I left the cafe and allowed the guy in front of the hotel to call over a cab for me. "Penn Station," I told the cabbie. Felt like that's all I had been saying to cabbies these days. But the deja vu went a lot deeper than that.

The cab got to the station in plenty of time. I looked at the board and noted the track for my train — to Wilmington. But I knew I wouldn't be seeing Ilana again on this train. I half-consciously touched my chest. No need for the specially woven vest, either. It wouldn't be waiting for me in the locker in Wilmington Station. My counterpart had already taken it, yesterday. And I had no need for it. I wouldn't be traveling through time, this time.

I boarded the train, and tried to make myself comfortable in my seat. But there would be not much comfort in this trip, not in my seat or my skin, and not much enjoyment in the clothes and colors and culture of 1970, either. That probably came from my discomfort at being a guinea pig, a pawn, of Ian's, rather than his client. But what did it matter? It's not as if his clients had much control over their destinies, either. And what choice did I have? Ian had a monopoly on the time travel which had become the lifeblood of my life, because I had made it that way.

I fidgeted when the train pulled into Philadelphia. This is where I had left my seat the other day on the way to the Cafe Car and its exit to the past. No need for the Cafe Car today. I was already in the past.

The train pulled out of Philadelphia and soon was in Wilmington. I left the train and caught a taxi. "Telegraph office," I instructed, and provided the address.

***

"It's an experimental process," Ian had explained to me, back in the hotel room. "My team has been working on it for years. The possibilities are profound, as you'll no doubt agree."

I had never seen Ian so ... eager ... so much the pitchman. But I agreed with his assessment. People could travel as far back as 1969 on the Tricela-Metroliner route. If this telegraph gambit worked, Ian's clients could eventually send telegrams from a few years before 2006 — when the last words-only telegram was sent out for hand delivery by Western Union — to as far back in time as 1848, when the central telegraph office started doing business in Wilmington, Delaware on Front and King Streets.

I tipped the cabbie copiously, and entered the Western Union office. There were two tellers, each with a line of customers. I got at the end of the shorter line and waited. Each of the three people in front of me sent money orders. The teller counted the bills in slow, exaggerated motions.

I finally stepped up to the teller. He had white hair and a ruddy face, and was likely in his early 60s. "I have an old-fashioned kind of telegram to send," I said, and laughed. "Just words, no money."

"Yes, sir."

I gave him a sheet of paper, on which the message I wished to send was carefully, and I hope clearly, printed.

"Can I read this to you, sir?" he inquired.

"Yes, please do," I replied.

The teller began. "Mr. Herbert George Wells, 123 Eardley Road, Sevenoaks, Kent, England," he read aloud. "Is that right for the name and address?"

"Yes." I could tell from his tone and demeanor — unless he was a world-class actor — that he'd never heard the name. Likely because the recipient of the telegram was better known by his first two initials, or maybe this teller was no fan of science fiction, who knew. But in any case it was a good thing, because it saved me the trouble of explaining why I was sending a telegram in 1970 to a man who had died in 1946.

The teller cleared his throat. I realized I had been staring at him. "And please read the message now," I said.

He complied. "Strongly urge you to bring Chronic Argonauts" — he stumbled slightly over the last word, but pronounced it tolerably well - "into full bloom as a novel STOP Will sell well STOP Will inspire you to write other novels STOP Indeed a device just aborning called the wireless telegraph as per Tesla and Lodge will later help greatly with sales of those novels STOP You will thank me for this many years later when we speak together through this wireless for an interview"—

I nodded that that was the message. I enjoyed hearing the word STOP — Ian, ever the penny pincher, would likely have instructed me to use it instead of the period in any case, since punctuation was charged for, but STOP was a Western Union freebie. But that was not the reason he had included it in this message, every word of which he had dictated to me, without even going through the motions of making sure I agreed that the content worked with what I knew of H. G. Wells. Fortunately, I thought that it did.

"Ok," the teller said. "And you would like this signed, 'An American admirer with a similar name'."

"Yes."

"That's a little long for a signature," the teller said.

"That's the way I want it," I replied. "You can charge me for it," I added, helpfully.

"You pay for every word, Sir, except the STOP used in lieu of the period."

Charming. But no wonder the telegram had gone the way of hieroglyphics.

***

I stepped out of the office into the street and the heat. The late afternoon sun was even worse than in New York. Not surprising — I was, after all, further south.

But Ian was perpetually surprising. What he hoped to accomplish with this telegraph connection to the past, and how he thought it would work, had truly floored me.

"You can't change so much as a letter in the telegram," he had instructed me. "No ad libbing, as you might be tempted to do in your craft of acting."

So he's a critic, too, I had thought. But I had permitted myself a question. "Why?"

Ian had looked at me for a few moments, as if sizing me up as to whether I could understand what he was about to tell me. He apparently concluded that I could. "It's not the precise sense of the words that I most care about. It's the electronic signal that their commission to the telegraph will produce."

"I'm not sure I understand." Though I thought I had an inkling of where he was going with this.

Ian obliged me. "The Morse Code, in addition to its translatability into these words — based, of course, on the arbitrary assignment of electronic signals to letters — will also have an effect that is not arbitrary at all. That signal, and only that specific, exact signal, will both connect into the temporal anomaly north of Wilmington, the one that made your travel to here possible—"

"Right," I said.

"—that signal, and only that specific, exact signal," he repeated, with a glare for my interruption, "will not only be sent across the sea to England — as any telegram could be sent today in 1970 — but, because of its entwinement with the Wilmington anomaly, will ignite its sending to England in 1894."

"Was there even transatlantic cable in 1894?" I asked.

"It was laid down right after the U.S. Civil War. A major engineering feat of its day."

"So the specific signal is the equivalent of the vest," I had mused. "The precise Morse code signal is the equivalent of the weave."

"Yes."

"To move not people but information back in time," I said.

"Yes."

"Information back in time to H. G. Wells," I said.

"Yes," Ian replied, now monosyllabic.

I took it in, as best I could. "But ... why?"

***

I had known the answer to that would require a lot more than one word. How much Ian chose to tell me, of course, was another matter ...

I stopped my reverie and looked around for a cab. Would it be air conditioned? Yes! Lucky break at last, and a hell of a lot better than this wilting Wilmington heat.

"Wilmington Station," I told the driver.

"I have quite a lucrative business," Ian had replied to my question, back in my hotel room, "as you no doubt have gathered. H. G. Wells's *Time Machine*, though pretty far in the past, was a necessary start-up factor."

"Because it got the world thinking about time travel?"

"That's right," Ian had replied. "Oh, there were a few stories before, but *The Time Machine* really put time travel on the intellectual map. Without any intervention from me, Wells would likely have expanded "The Chronic Argonauts" story into *The Time Machine* novel anyway — his biographers say he was hungry for a larger audience — but I'm thinking a little extra nudge can't hurt, a little insurance that history does the right thing for me."

I had looked at Ian. Behind his meticulous, scowling confidence was a bit more insecurity than I would have expected.

And he had smiled back at me, genuinely, for an instant. "Yes, there's no such thing as too much of a good thing when it comes to making sure history is on your side."

***

My cab arrived at the Wilmington station. I paid the cabbie and took the shaky elevator up to the northbound platform. God, it seemed as it was more than two lifetimes ago when I had been in this dingy, odiferous box. But that was, what, just two days ago?

I had had one last question of Ian, back at the Barclay in New York just yesterday.

"Why me?" I had asked Ian. "Why do you need *me* to send the telegram to H. G. Wells?"

"I've done this myself — used that office in Wilmington to send telegrams to the past — and the process worked fine. But you have some sort of cosmic entwinement with H. G. Wells -- the closeness of your names, your intersection with him in the early part of your career, convinced me that you were the ideal person to send this extraordinary telegram. For all I've been able to do with time travel, I still think of it as a toddler that needs all the support it can get.

"Bring Western Union — Western Un-ion — into Ian's Ions and Eons," I mused, and pronounced the second word as "un" and "ion" to make my point.

"That's right," Ian had said, "though I prefer the French pronunciation of 'un' - meaning 'one,' or one with the ions."

***

My train arrived. I had to remind myself again that I wouldn't be time traveling on this one — it was 1970 now, and it would be 1970 when I reached New York.

But I had sent information back in time, to H. G. Wells, in 1894. I took a seat by the window, and looked out, as my train slid out of the station. Yeah, it had apparently worked with me — Ian had gotten what we wanted. After all, I was here on this train in 1970, I had come back here from the future, after booking my trip in Ian's Ions and Eons, and my heart felt fine.

But the impact of this message to the past had been only to buttress what my almost namesake Herbert George Wells had already been on his way to doing, anyway. And as I looked out at the rapidly receding shrubs and rust of the Wilmington train station, I had to wonder: now that I had helped Ian validate this process, what would happen when he sold people the means of sending messages to the past intended not to support but change or undo history? Would Ian do that?

"Excuse me — are you Orson Welles?" a leggy brunette, with a high, stylish, mauve mini-skirt or some such asked me.

"Yes," I replied, not very warmly. If I hadn't been so engrossed in thinking about Ian, I might have invited her to sit down next to me.

She started to turn—

"Care to join me?" I asked her, in the most inviting baritone I could muster. I gestured to the empty seat next to me.

Her eyes lit up. "Yes, thank you!" She sat down. "I saw you on the Dick Cavett Show night before last — you were very clever, Mr. Welles."

"Call me George," I said. "It comes before the Orson."

She smiled. "I'm Isabella."

ROBINSON
CALCULATOR

First published by Connected Editions, *July 2019*.

1

I first noticed the name on a headstone in the Woodlawn Cemetery in the Bronx – "Robinson Calculator".

I mean, would they be so blatant – to bury one of their own under a tombstone which plainly identified the deceased as "Calculator"? That would bring hiding in plain sight to a whole new level.

I'm not making this up. You'd see this with your own eyes if you were in the right spot in the cemetery. I'd understand if you didn't – most people are only visiting the cemetery because they're grieving for a loved one. But sometimes there's less grief than other times – you know, for a member of the family by marriage, and you didn't really know the old guy all that well. And if there were no tears in your eyes, and you looked in the right place – trust me, you'd see that name incised in stone, too. "Robinson Calculator".

I've been tracking those people for years – though, obviously, they're not really people. And the sight of that name on the headstone was a shard of ice in my heart. Because it meant they didn't care anymore, didn't worry about who saw them or knew about them.

***

I have nothing against them. In fact, I like them – they have spunk and style. My friend – a college buddy – had been married to one. That was the only reason I knew about them. Most people had no idea Calculators even existed. Dave's wife didn't use her maiden name.

I chuckled to myself. "Maiden" doesn't seem quite right for a Calculator, does it? Doesn't seem quite right for anyone anymore, but I liked this particular Calculator – hell, more than that, I'd wanted her. I'd been very attracted to her. I had mixed feelings when they broke up. Dave and Lianne had planned on adopting, but he had become increasingly obsessed with seeing his DNA come to life in a new being, and of course there was no way that could happen with Lianne.

I had been on the verge of contacting her a bunch times in the few years since they'd split, but seeing that name on the headstone gave me new impetus.

***

Just to be clear, I know that people have all kinds of last names derived from real objects, and I don't think for a minute that the holders of names derived from objects are endowed with the physical properties of those objects. I mean, no one looked for gold or water when they saw Barry Goldwater – though for all I knew, he sported a gold ring or watch, and his body was certainly made of whatever big percentage of water, like all human beings.

Hey, there was a girl by the name of Samantha Sugar in my high school bio class, and I surely didn't think she was literally sweet – though she did have a sweet smile when she wanted to show it and a sweet ass, too, in those snug cotton jeans.

But the Calculators were something else. The name apparently originated in Europe, as far back as the Golem and the real automata that preceded the mythical Golem by centuries. Heron of ancient Alexandria had constructed automata far earlier, though there is no surviving evidence that he called them Calculator as a last name, or anything at all. They mostly had only one name back then, anyway, right?

But the Calculators were different. Whenever they originated, they started "life" as a family, a big family, with aunts and uncles as well as parents and children. And the family grew. With first and last names, and the last name was always Calculator.

***

I texted Lianne Calculator. "How are you doing?"

"Wow! Wild to hear from you! I'm watching *Battlestar Galactica*. Never gets old," she replied.

Figured. I caught my breath. I was surprised by how good it felt to be in touch with her again. "Hey, how about lunch in the next few days – Blue Ribbon Sushi on Sullivan Street?" I knew she lived in the Village and worked from home. I also knew Dave hated sushi and she loved it.

"Sure," she replied. "How does Thursday sound to you?"

***

I ordered the big orange clam and she ordered the sweet ebi. We talked for a few minutes about inconsequential things.

Then she took my hand. "I'm not ready yet for anything more than friendship."

"Ok."

"I know you're the kind of guy who thinks if she doesn't want my dick she doesn't want my soul, but–"

My mouth hung open. I filled it with a piece of clam. I guess that's what I meant by spunk.

"Do you think I have a soul?" she shifted focus. "Seriously."

"In a religious sense?" I sipped some sencha tea, grateful for the change of topic. "I'm not sure I know what that means. If it's something that God supposedly breathed into human beings, well, then I'm agnostic. If it's just a word for what my brain contains, then, yeah, I think you're my mental equal. I wouldn't think you were any different from me at all, if your name were not …"

"Calculator?"

"Right," I said. "Why do you use it?"

"It's the law," Lianne replied.

I laughed. "What law would that be? The politicos know about you?"

"Common law," Lianne said. "Goes back centuries."

"Ah, ok – so it's some kind of profound, deeply embedded custom."

She gave me a look. "I don't know if I'd call it 'profound'." She bit into one of the crunchy fried shells of her shrimp, which had been served to her so quickly that its appearance on our table almost seemed surreptitious.

"But it's an important custom," I said.

She nodded and crunched away.

"Who came up with it – was it imposed on you?" I asked her.

She cleared her palate and throat with tea. "We did ... why are you suddenly so interested?"

I told her about Robinson Calculator in the cemetery.

"Never heard of him," she said and summoned the waiter. "I'll have another ebi."

"I'm fine," I said to the waiter. And to Lianne, "Do you know all the Calculators?"

Now she laughed. "Of course not. Do you know all the human beings?" Her laughter sounded like rain. I like rain. That Beatles song has always been one of my favorites. I sang a bar of "Rain" under my breath. I'd heard it just yesterday on Peter Asher's show on Sirius XM Radio.

"I assume there aren't as many Calculators as humans, right?" I said and summoned another waiter. "More tea please." I looked at Lianne, who nodded. "For both of us."

The waiter quickly bowed and left.

"No, we aren't as numerous as humans," Lianne said, in slow, mockingly exaggerated tones. "But I doubt you know anything close to the names of every human even in your neighborhood or on your block."

I nodded.

"And the only reason you know about me – about my kind – is I was married to Dave," Lianne added.

The original waiter returned with Lianne's ebi and a pot of tea. He refilled our cups. "Anything more?" he asked, politely.

I shook my head no. "When do you think your people made a decision to put one of their names on such a publicly viewable tombstone?" I asked Lianne.

She considered for a moment. "I don't know that they did. I mean, I believe you about what you saw on that tombstone, but I don't know if that was the result of a decision by the Calculators."

"I took a picture of it," I said and reached for my phone.

"I believe you," Lianne said again.

"Ok," I said, and looked down for a moment at my tea. The

pale green liquid seemed to shimmer in my cup, as if, I don't know, in response to some soft sound wave. Then I realized there was indeed sound in the room, or at least at our table. Lianne was singing. And she was somehow singing all the parts to the song, all the harmony, so softly that only I could hear.

I looked around at the people at the other tables. They couldn't hear her. It was like I was wearing earbuds and Lianne was in the phone. It was beautiful. B. J. Thomas's "Rock 'n' Roll Lullaby". She was singing it just for me.

My father had loved that song, especially those Blossom and Beach Boy harmonies. He had sung more than half of those harmonies as we walked the beach on the bay side of Cape Cod. I knew I'd never told Lianne about that – hell, I doubt I ever told Dave.

Lianne smiled at me and stopped singing. "I researched you.

"After I texted you about lunch?"

"After the first time I met you, when I was with Dave," she replied.

Now *I* smiled. She was very distracting. "You think human beings put the name Calculator on that headstone?" I asked her. I wanted to stay focused.

Lianne sucked on her ebi sushi. Her eyes closed in appreciation. She sang the chorus almost in a whisper.

She obviously didn't want to discuss this. I sipped my tea.

"It began to become public in the 1920s," Lianne suddenly said. "It all began to change with *R.U.R.*"

"Karol Čapek's play? *Rossum's Universal Robots*?"

"Yeah," Lianne said. "That's when robots first entered the popular culture in a big way – got Asimov going, and Data, and *Westworld* and everything else. Čapek gave robots their name."

"Did Čapek know about you?" I asked.

"About the Calculators? I don't know – I wasn't alive back then." It occurred to me that I knew nothing about Calculator lifespans. "How old are you? I mean–"

She squeezed my hand. I had touched her hand before, and I knew it was warm, but for some reason I was a little surprised by its warmth now anyway.

"I enjoyed this," she said and stood. "How much do I owe you?"

She fished for her phone.

The waiter had yet to bring the bill. "On me," I said. "But– I hope I didn't offend you with anything I said–"

"You didn't," she said, and leaned over and kissed me on the lips to prove it. I believed her, and thought, well, Dave was even more of a fool than I'd thought he'd been to leave her.

I watched her walk to the front of the restaurant. If it walks like a duck and talks like a duck ... well, she sure walked like a woman.

***

I paid the bill and took the D train up to Central Park. Walking in the park helped me think.

The key point in understanding Lianne and her people – yeah, they seemed like people to me, even though I knew that technically they weren't – was that they had been around a long time. Our digital age and the decades before get all the credit – at least the public credit – for robots and AI. And Alexa and Siri and all of that are indeed 21st century. But Charles Babbage had started it all back in the 1820s, with his Difference Engine. And that was more than just a fanciful design – a working Difference Engine had actually been constructed at the Science Museum in London around 1990, if memory served.

So Babbage's designs worked, at least for very primitive computer calculators. Could they have been responsible for the Calculators – or someone building off his work, like Ada Lovelace? Had they given the name Calculator to an actual body made of flesh and blood and some sort of primitive electric circuitry? Well, according to Lianne Calculator, no, the Calculators existed long before Babbage. Could I believe her about that? If she was telling the truth, the Calculators likely had happened the other way around, with Babbage and Lovelace jumping on the work of someone else, some "mute, inglorious Milton" of computing, as my favorite line in that sad Thomas Gray poem had it about geniuses who died without ever achieving any notice or fame. Except this Milton likely had lived long before the real John Milton and his *Paradise Lost*.

But if the Calculators owed their origin to someone else, then whom? Some person, or going further back, some civilization that left no other traces of its existence, or none that we knew of?

Yeah, walks in the park helped me think. Sometimes too much.

2

It was time to see Dave. He was the best source that I knew, other than Lianne herself, with detailed knowledge of the Calculators. And, given that Lianne seemed to have an agenda of some sort all her own, Dave could be helpful.

He was easy enough to find and meet. He was a Professor of Philosophy at the New School, down on 14th Street in the north end of the Village.

I texted him with a lunch invitation. It felt a little weird, proposing lunch with Dave the day after lunch with his ex-wife Lianne, but I didn't feel like waiting, and the weirdness still would have been there a week or a month from now.

"Sure," Dave replied. "I'm at Bobst Library, doing some research. It's at NYU, off Washington Square Park. You know where that is, right?"

"I do."

"How about we meet out front in two hours – around 1pm?"

"Great," I said. "See you then."

Dave was like that. First time we'd been in touch in several years, and he says sure, just like that. Well, we'd studied philosophy together on the other side of the pond over at the London School of Economics, and that kind of experience can bond you for life.

***

I walked up to meet him in front of Bobst at the appointed time. The New School and NYU had reciprocal library privileges once again, if I remembered correctly. Fordham University, where I taught up in the Bronx, did not. On the other hand, we had a pretty deep and well-stocked library, still a great resource, even in this digital age, with a fair number of books from the last two centuries that had not yet been scanned and put online.

Dave looked pretty much the same as the last time I'd seen him, a tad more paunchy, and grey in his hair.

"Jonathan," he clapped me on the back and shook my hand,

"you look exactly the same."

"You too! What's your pleasure for lunch?"

"How about Blue Ribbon Sushi – about a five-minute walk from here, on the other side of Houston Street."

I'd learned a long time ago there was no point in fighting coincidence, if that's what this was. "Sure."

We walked a few steps. "Would you believe I had lunch in that very same restaurant with Lianne just yesterday?" I said to Dave.

"Really? Yes, I'd believe it – she's crazy about sushi," Dave said. "Ironically, I developed a taste for it myself after our divorce.... What are you, making some kind of movie about us for that film and philosophy class you were teaching, and this is your research?" He laughed.

Good to see he wasn't angry. "You know me too well! I've actually been thinking about doing that, and I now have a connection at Netflix. But you know I've always been interested in the Calculators. And I saw a name, 'Robinson Calculator,' carved on a headstone, plain as day, a few days ago at Woodlawn Cemetery in the Bronx."

"Hmm, that *is* interesting," Dave said. "When I was with Lianne, they made a big deal about staying off the radar."

"Exactly," I said. "That's why I found the tombstone so unusual." I showed him the picture on my phone.

He looked at it carefully. "First time I've ever seen anything like that."

***

We reached the restaurant. The hostess recognized me and beamed, apparently honored that I'd come back the very next day for another lunch.

I was glad to see the orange clam was still on the "specials" menu. I ordered it again. As I used to tell my ex-wife, when I find something I like, I stick with it.

Dave looked at me and ordered the same. Our tea arrived.

"You know, probably the main reason we broke up is Lianne always felt I was studying her, even in bed." He sipped his tea and shook his head.

"Were you?" I might as well see where this went, if he was raising the subject.

"Of course. Wouldn't you? Isn't that why you're here?"

I answered bluntness with bluntness. "What is she made of, inside? If you don't mind my asking. I mean, did you ever see any x-rays or body scans of her?"

"She stayed strictly away from doctors," Dave replied. "For obvious reasons."

I nodded. "She never got sick?"

"She had some allergies in the summer. A cold every once in a while," Dave said. "But nothing that ever drove her to seek medical attention – as far I know. We were only married for three-and-a-half years."

Our food arrived. I shook my head a little, in disbelief. "How did they have the knowledge back then to create someone like Lianne?"

Dave was a philosopher. I knew he welcomed such questions.

"I honestly don't know," he said. "She refused to ever talk about it. And I couldn't find anything in any research. "But … "

Our waiter returned with a teapot. "More tea?"

"Yes," Dave said. He seemed glad to be interrupted.

"And?" I prodded. I wasn't about to let tea change the topic.

Dave sipped his refilled cup. "And, I don't know, I guess I wouldn't be totally shocked to find out that Lianne is as human as you or I, and the whole Calculator thing is some kind of hoax."

***

I took my phone out of my pocket and showed him the photo again. "You think that's a hoax?" I also thought about that multiple harmony she had sung for me in this very place, just yesterday, but, I don't know, it felt too personal for me to mention to him.

He barely glanced at the photo this time. "All that proves is that someone by the name of Robinson Calculator is buried there. It doesn't prove that he was some kind of android or robot or artificially constructed human, or that Lianne actually is, too."

"No, of course not," I said. "But what's the likelihood of my seeing that, out of the blue, years after knowing about you and Lianne, and what you were sure Lianne really was, at least then?"

Dave shook his head and said nothing.

I hadn't expected this.

He dug into his clam. I did the same. No point in pressing the conversation, in probing his literally intimate knowledge of Lianne any further, if it made him so uncomfortable. Maybe I'd been wrong to push it this far.

"You should talk to the blind professor," Dave eventually said. "He's a bit of a Brooklyn hipster but a specialist on everything from the Golem to the Frankenstein monster."

**

I caught up with Professor Rodney Rodriguez – Dave's "blind professor" – at a science fiction convention the following week in Westchester County. He wore thick dark glasses and was, indeed, blind. Appropriately, he was introducing a 1920 movie of *The Golem – Der Golem, wie er in die Welt kam* – "The Golem, as he came into the world". Joe Rapsis, a musician from Bedford, New Hampshire, provided musical effects on a keyboard. With all of my focus on names these days, I wondered if he was also into rap music.

Rodriguez provided a vivid and knowledgeable context for the film. His body shook as he talked, and somehow that seemed totally apt and natural. "The essence of the Golem, and of all its predecessors and successors, is life from non-life. The original Adam was a kind of golem, right? He was created from dust. The Golem of Chelm from the late 1500s was created from some kind of inanimate matter. The famous Golem of Prague a few years later was made from clay – he is the basis of our movie tonight. But speaking of Prague, it's no coincidence that Karel Čapek, a Czech, wrote *R. U. R.* in 1920. And Asimov's robots followed some twenty years later – all life from nonlife."

"I thought the robot stories are about artificial intelligence, not artificial life," some guy with unkempt long grey hair who looked like a golem himself called out from the front row, though no one had called for questions.

"The two go hand in hand in robots," Rodriguez replied, pleased to get the comment. "Robots move through the world – they're not disembodied brains in a vat or programs in a computer. They're intelligent because they're alive. That's why they're a kind of golem."

I figured what the hell and raised my own hand. Then I

realized Rodriguez couldn't see it. "Is there any indication of who created the golem in his various forms," I asked. "We know that Asimov's robots were invented by his character Susan Calvin, right?"

"Good question," Rodriguez replied. "The golems were created by rabbis – but their creation was more an act of magic than science or invention. By the way, Čapek 's robots were created from organic material, and were more like androids than robots – they could pass for strange humans, and didn't look like machines."

I hadn't known that. So the Calculators – Lianne, Robinson, and however many there were – were like the Čapek robots which predated Asimov's. And if they were even older, as Lianne had said, that meant that maybe Čapek knew about them, and had based his robots on the Calculators.

***

I stopped in Dobbs Ferry on the way home, to pick up a belt that I'd left in a shoe-repair shop. The loop needed repair, and I'd also needed some new holes punched into the belt, to accommodate the pounds I'd taken off, swimming at the New York Sports Club every day.

Something about this shop, I realized as I walked in, felt like it had relevance to the Calculators, even though I'd brought my belt into this place at least a week or more before I'd seen Robinson Calculator carved on the gravestone in the cemetery.

I'd actually almost forgotten about my belt – it had likely been ready since before the cemetery. I thought of that old joke and laughed to myself: A guy goes back to his old neighborhood, sees the old shoe-repair shop still in business on the corner. He walks into the shop, and the proprietor, some elderly craftsman from Italy or wherever, looks at him, walks into the back, comes out with a pair of shoes the visitor left in the store twenty or thirty years earlier and never picked up. Well, I hadn't waited that long, and the proprietor here was a Mr. Chen, but that's what this felt like.

Chen nodded, walked into the back of his shop, and returned a few long moments later with my belt. "I also sewed, it was coming loose," he said and pointed to the sewing on the edges of the belt.

"No charge!"

"Thank you," I replied and left the store. I'd already paid for the repair – four dollars, believe it or not – and I didn't want to insult the generosity of his sewing gift by insisting on paying for it. Ok, Chen and this kind of repair shop did have some relevance to my Robinson Calculator obsession. Given their antiquity, it was clear that the Calculators didn't emerge from some laboratory or assembly line. They no doubt were the product of craftsmen, tinkerers like Edison, like Mr. Chen, who took personal pride in their work.

Well, that's not to say that laboratory scientists don't take pride in what they do, and Thomas Edison was certainly not from antiquity or the Middle Ages, but there was something about the Calculators that whispered the pleasure of someone creating a lifelike statue out of stone or wood. Except the Calculators were more than lifelike. They were life, definitely some kind of life.

I decided on impulse to text Lianne again. I would never say she was lifelike. She was straight-up alive. Vibrantly living her life. I suddenly got what Dave had been trying to tell me. No craftsman or scientist could have made her. If anything, she was more the product of some insanely powerful magic, like the Golem. But that didn't seem like an explanation for her existence, either – or not an explanation I was inclined to accept. It certainly wouldn't play as well as secret science in the movie I was indeed thinking more and more about making.

I needed to know Lianne better – I needed to know what Dave had known. She had told me point blank that she didn't want anything more than friendship between us, right now, but—

"How about dinner, this time?" I messaged her.

"Love to," she replied instantly. "When and where?"

***

We met at the Lido Restaurant in Harlem three nights later. Sushi wasn't the only food I liked, and she apparently felt the same way.

I got the warm kale salad with shrimp, she got the duck something or other. We talked about superficial things, just as we had at the start of the last meal we'd shared. This was all my fault, this time, not hers. I was relishing the normal banter and the dinner too much to spoil it with questions about the nature of her existence.

We finished the first bottle of wine before dessert. I asked her if she wanted more.

She smiled and shook her head no. "You're wondering if alcohol affects Calculators the same as humans, right?"

"No, I was just asking—"

"It does--," Lianne began, just as the waiter approached and asked if we wanted another bottle of wine.

"No," we both turned and began, and Lianne's elbow tipped over a full glass of water, a glass with a very thin stem.

"Not to worry," the waiter said, and went off to get some napkins.

The water was all over the table and Lianne's lap. Ever the gentleman, I started patting the table dry, while Lianne patted her lap. *You're wondering if we rust*, I heard her say in my mind's ear, *well we don't.* In reality, she laughed, a really nice laugh, and said, "I'm such a klutz."

"No, you're not," I said, and looked up from the table to her lips, and kissed them.

She kissed me back and twirled her tongue around mine. "Our kind lies, too," she said, when we came up for air. "And we change our minds."

The waiter approached with napkins.

"We're ok," I told him.

"Like when I said I didn't want to be more than friends," she finished her thought, softly.

"Would you like the dessert menu?" the waiter asked.

I looked at Lianne. "We'll take the check," I told the waiter.

***

We Ubered up to my apartment in Inwood.

"Nice view of the river," Lianne said, but that was the last we looked out of the window that evening.

I'm not sure if it was the best sex I ever had, but it was right up there. These things are non-comparable, anyway.

"I love you," I almost said. I was sure I hadn't actually said that, and yet—

"The testicles of the male quail are twice the size of its heart,"

Lianne murmured.

And she soon was asleep on my chest, softly snoring.

I gently stroked her back, and tried to make some sense of this. I kept coming back to what Dave had implied. What difference did it make, whether she was human, or somehow constructed to be indistinguishable from a human in all important ways, maybe in all ways.

Well, not in every way. I didn't have to worry about using a condom, or asking her if she was on some kind of birth control.

But that wasn't a defining characteristic of every human, either – there were, after all, some women who couldn't get pregnant, some men and some women who couldn't conceive.

She'd come, twice. I liked the sound of her voice like that. It was as human as it came.

What if the only significant difference between Calculators and humans was that humans constantly wondered about the humanlike characteristics of Calculators – how they were just like us, how they were very different from us? I fell asleep with Lianne in my arms, thinking about her face, not my movie.

***

I awoke the next morning. Lianne was gone. She'd left a note on her pillow, like in a dozen television shows.

"Had a great time," the note said. "Had an early appointment. Let's do again."

It occurred to me that I had no idea what Lianne did – I knew she worked at home, but I had never talked to her or Dave about what that work was. In all of our conversations, in all of my questions about who or what she essentially was, what she did for a living hadn't come up.

I decided to take a walk in the park – this time, Inwood Hill Park, a few feet from my apartment building. Yeah, I hadn't yet lost faith in the ability of walks in the park to help me think. The sun was bright, and the air was rich with late Spring pollen. Fortunately, I wasn't allergic. It was all good.

I was a professor of philosophy and a filmmaker, but also an amateur historian. Maybe not so amateur. The history of knowledge, an intrinsic part of epistemology, was inevitably a study of history, too.

I and many others had always wondered about the spark that had gotten our civilization going. The Chinese, the Arabs, many cultures had made great discoveries, and accomplished great things. But there was something about the Greek and Roman combination that had ultimately ignited the science and technology that had lifted us off this planet, had cracked the code of life, and, yeah, had created apps which certainly had a lot of the characteristics of human intelligence – apps that answered questions, provided instructions, apps you could practically fall in love with, if you weren't careful.

And Lianne had presumably come out of that human mode of invention – unless the Chinese or some other non-Greco-Roman civilization had some incredible expertise in flesh-and-blood artificial intelligence that had been hidden from the rest of the world.

But maybe there was another way of looking at this – could Lianne and the Calculators have come not from the distant past but the distant or not-so-distant future? That would explain why we had no knowledge of who created the Calculators – how could we have knowledge of circumstances of creation which hadn't happened yet?

But that possibility – that the Calculators had come here to our past from our future – required time travel. And travel to the past engendered paradoxes which were far more insurmountable than the unaccountable existence of human-like androids. If I traveled to the past to change something and changed it, how would I have had the knowledge of what to change in the first place? The multi-worlds hypothesis, that every time the time-traveler changed something in the past, a new world was brought into being, could help at least a little with that problem. Jonathan1 from World1 travels to the past and changes something. This brings into being World2, where that event didn't happen, and Jonathan2 had no knowledge of it. So there's no paradox, because the time traveler was Jonathan1 not Jonathan2. A cool way of getting out of the paradox, but, let's face it, a new world coming into being with every drop of the time traveler's hat was a state of affairs even more incredible than time travel itself.

And time travel to the future had its own set of crazy issues.

If I traveled to tomorrow and was lucky enough to see Lianne in those same lavender panties she'd had on last night, did that mean she'd have no choice tomorrow but to wear those lavender panties? What if black was her preference tomorrow morning? What happened to her free will?

Ok, so Lianne coming from the future might remove the questions of what kind of civilization created her in the past, and how come we didn't know about it, but coming from the future saddled us with problems that were far worse.

I looked across the Hudson at the Palisades. There was a theory floating around – not really a theory, more like pure speculation – that the Palisades had been carved whole out of the rocks by some alien civilization from the stars. Could the Calculators be the result of some alien visitation to Earth, eons ago?

Well, that would explain why there was no known human civilization with that kind of technology, but what other evidence did we have of such an alien visitation?

There was a professor in the Comm Department at Fordham – Kathleen Harney – who had some expertise in that area. She'd given a paper a few years ago at a faculty seminar on the correlation between intensity of religious belief and belief in UFOs, and had found in her surveys, I guess surprisingly, that fundamentalists were more likely to believe in extraterrestrials than were atheists, agnostics, and people with casual religious beliefs. I rarely if ever attended those seminars – a colleague in my department had twisted my arm to come and hear this – but I'd really enjoyed Harney's presentation—

My phone beeped with a text. It was from Lianne. "U up for lunch today? Someone I'd like u to meet. I saw a nice-looking restaurant around the corner from your apartment building."

3

The Indian Road Café was much better than it should have been. Located on the ground floor of a big old shapeless apartment building that took up most of the block, much like mine, just a few steps from mine. But its food and drink were delicious – a little American, a little Japanese, a little this and that – and Inwood Hill Park was right across the street.

I got to the Café around 5 minutes to 1pm – about 5 minutes earlier than our arranged meeting time, unusual for me. I looked around the Café and breathed in the usual welcome aromas, mostly coffee with a hint of some kind of liqueur. Lianne was not yet here, but a man caught my eye. He half stood, and waved me over to his table.

He looked something like Timothy Leary, with long, slightly messy, white and grey hair. (If you don't know what that looks like, look him up on Google.)

"Jonathan?" he said to me, and gestured to a chair. The table seated four.

I obliged and took a seat. "I assume you're the one Lianne wanted me to meet?"

He nodded and sipped a beer. It was light, but otherwise, I'm no expert on beer.

"And you are?" I asked.

A waiter came by. "What are you drinking?" he asked me.

"Iced tea," I replied.

"Ok," the waiter said. "Ready to order?" he asked me and included 'Timothy' in his question.

"We're expecting one more person," I replied.

"Lianne won't be coming," 'Timothy' said.

"What?" I asked sharply, confused and not happy.

The waiter started to ask us again if we were ready to order but thought the better of it. "I'll come back in a few minutes for your order. Would you like another one?" he asked my companion, who had emptied his mug.

"I'm fine, thanks," he replied.

The waiter nodded and walked away.

"What do you mean, she's not coming?" I demanded, in a quiet voice that barely concealed my displeasure.

"She had an unexpected engagement," 'Timothy' replied.

"Where?"

"I don't know," 'Timothy' said, and raised his hands in a soothing gesture.

I didn't buy it. "And you are?" I repeated my earlier question, unanswered due to the waiter's arrival.

"Unimportant," he said.

So my question would have been unanswered in any case. "Look—" I began.

"I know," he said, "you came here to see Lianne."

"Right," I said, and looked at my phone. I began to text her.

"She's not likely to answer you," 'Timothy' replied.

I messaged her anyway, and stared at the phone, waiting for her reply. I got nothing. I couldn't even be sure, with this phone, if she'd received my text.

The waiter came by with my tea.

"We still need a few more minutes," 'Timothy' informed him.

"Of course," the waiter said, and walked away.

"I assure you, she's fine," the man across the table told me, anticipating my question.

But I wasn't reassured in the slightest. "Look—" I began again.

"My last name is Calculator," he interrupted me, again. "And my first name is John. Does that help put you at ease?"

"No, not really," I replied. "John is probably the most common name in the English language. It's practically my name, too." Not to mention that he'd just said he was a Calculator.

John laughed. It wasn't as melodic as Lianne's. "I can't help what my name is," he said. "I didn't choose it."

"Who did?"

"Long story," John said, "and I don't want to take up too much of your time. Let me tell you why I wanted to meet you. You're very interested in the Calculators, I know. You think you saw a name on a tombstone—"

"I don't think that, I know that," I said, with some heat now, and went to my photos on my phone. "What the hell—" The photo of the tombstone was gone. Could this John have somehow erased it, as I was sitting here word-sparring with him?

"Let me be brief," John said. "I know you like Lianne, and she likes you. But this is not a good time for the two of you … to get involved. Take my advice. Back off. Let this breathe. You're both young, there'll be plenty of time for the two of you later."

"Who exactly are you, her father?"

John smiled wanly, reached into his wallet, and stood, He put a 20-dollar bill on the table. "This should cover our beverages."

"Are you a Calculator leader?" I asked him.

"Give it time. Trust me. You'll get the answers you seek." And he walked towards the door.

"Ready to order now?" our waiter returned and asked.

"This will be it," I replied and gestured to the twenty dollars on the table. "Keep the change."

I walked quickly to the door, intending to catch up with John. But three mothers with twice as many little kids were entering the café at just that moment.

I got outside a few crucial seconds later. I looked in every direction. There was no sign of John.

***

I half ran to the elevated train on Broadway. I could take that to 242nd Street in the Bronx, and Uber from there to Woodlawn Cemetery.

The train took longer than usual to arrive, the clanking on the tracks was painfully slow, and even the Uber took twice as long as indicated to pick me up. Nothing was going right for me today.

I eventually got to the cemetery. I knew exactly where the Robinson Calculator tombstone was located. I walked there as quickly as I could without attracting attention.

Easy enough to take another photo of that tombstone, as many pics as I wanted. Whatever or whoever had erased my first photo had also deleted it from my cloud. I realized that this could have been Lianne's handiwork, when I was blissfully unconscious last night. I really preferred not to think that. But I hadn't a clue about how John might have managed to do it. If it indeed had been him – if he had somehow erased my photo on my phone and on my cloud when I'd been sitting there, furious that Lianne was not there, not paying any attention at first to my phone – then this bespoke powers of the Calculators I'd never heard of or thought about. But I still wanted to believe it was not Lianne, setting me up with great sex, taking advantage when I was sound asleep beside her.

I saw the tombstone in the distance. I could see immediately that there would be no photo today. And, I had a sinking feeling, on any day. The tombstone was draped, and two men were busily at work on it, in what appeared to be some kind of sandblasting action.

I approached them as non-aggressively as I could. A third man approached us from the side. Some kind of security. "Please, sir," he said to me, in an Eastern European accent, "let the men work. Do not disturb them. We always must have respect for the dead."

They were erasing what was on that tombstone. Robinson Calculator. I couldn't let them do that. I spoke up: "I'm a member of the family. Robinson's son. We didn't give you permission to do that." I took a step closer.

The security guard did the same. We were face to face. "You have identification, please?"

"Sure," I made a point of fumbling with my wallet. I could rush the tombstone, brush aside the drapery, and photograph whatever was still left on it—

But I saw two cops out of the corner of my eye, leisurely walking in our direction. Whether they were here to grieve, or on routine patrol, or as additional security, I had no way of knowing. My security guard saw where I was looking, turned to look at the police, then turned back to me. "You have identification?" he said to me again.

The sandblasting continued. If I pushed past the guard to get to the tombstone, I'd definitely be arrested, likely for assault. That wouldn't do me or my quest the slightest good.

The sandblasting stopped. The workers removed the drape. Just as I'd feared. There was now no lettering at all on the smooth, gleaming face of the tombstone. Just some residual dust.

I sighed and backed off. "I must've forgotten it, left it at home," I said quickly, and turned to walk away. Now I had nothing of Robinson Calculator. Not the tombstone, not my photograph. What was left?

4

Over the years, since I'd first begun looking into the Calculators, since I'd first met Lianne through Dave, I'd discovered a few places online that published various theories and speculations about the Calculators. As I waited for my Uber to take me back to the 242nd Street station, I tried to get to those sites on my phone. The little screen struggled and spun. Either the service here wasn't up to par – unlikely with four out of five bars of service – or those sites also had been eliminated.

I confirmed that when I got home, sitting near the window with a big potted snake plant and my laptop. Even the Wikipedia page on androids, which I was pretty sure had a line or two about the Calculators last time I'd looked at it, was bereft of any references to Lianne's people. Not only that, but there was no indication in the History section of the page that those lines had been removed, or had ever been there in the first place. If I correctly understood how Wikipedia worked, that must have taken some doing. More of John Calculator's intervention? This was beginning to strike me as more than the work of one man – or one Calculator. What the hell was I up against?

I sighed and shook my head. What did I have left about the Calculators?

Apparently, nothing. Nothing digital, nothing carved in stone. Nothing.

That left, what?

Flesh and blood, that's what it left.

I tried Lianne again and got the same lack of result. No response in text, audio, or FaceTime.

I drummed my fingers on the table, and tried the next best. I called Dave.

"Hey Jonathan," he answered.

I exhaled with some relief. At least Dave hadn't gone incommunicado. "I've been trying to get in touch with Lianne," I got right to the point, "and no luck on FaceTime, phone, or message," I told him. "I just wanted to make sure she was all right – sorry to bother you."

"Oh, no bother at all," Dave said. "She's like that. Sometimes she just goes underground. But I spoke to her today, about three or four hours ago, and she seemed fine."

That would have been right around the time she'd texted me about meeting her and John in the Indian Road Café. "I didn't know you were back in touch with her," I said, a little more stridently than I'd intended. "Sorry, I don't mean to hold you to account about Lianne – you certainly have every right—"

"It's ok," Dave replied. "Talking to you stirred some memories, and feelings. You actually have nothing to apologize about."

"I'm glad," I said. "Hey, apropos our good conversations, you up for lunch again today? My treat."

"Love to," Dave said. "But I've got a pain-in-the-ass departmental meeting today – bane of my existence."

"Tell me about it. My sympathies," I said

"Thanks," Dave said. "And I'm tied up all day tomorrow with classes."

"No problem," I said. "I'll let you go prepare for that meeting, and we can touch base later this week for lunch."

***

I resumed my finger-drumming on the table. No Internet, no tombstone, no people I could talk to who could help me. What was the point in talking to Kathleen Harney about an outer-space origin of the Calculators when I no longer had evidence of them here on Earth? Same for the blind professor and the Golem, and Chen in Dobbs Ferry.

But I had a feeling I was overlooking something. I scrolled through my email. Nothing relevant and – ah, here it was. An email forwarded to me and everyone in our Department a week ago about the New York Public Library main branch. They were finally re-opening their massive stacks – which had been under reconstruction, and open and closed for the past few years – and Fordham University faculty had privileges.

I made sure my university ID was in my wallet, dashed out of my apartment, and fast-walked to the A train. Someone was playing the Beatles' "Helter Skelter" out of a car – the 2018 remix, which was my favorite. It seemed appropriate to how I was feeling and what I was doing today.

The subway was fast and easy. I got out at 42nd Street, and walked quickly to Fifth Avenue and those iconic lions that stood stately guard at the entrance to the library. I'd been in the stacks a few times in my life. My Uncle Morty had worked there when he was a student at City College in the 1960s. Easy train ride for him, too, 125th Street down to 42nd Street via the D train.

He'd told me all sorts of stories about the stacks. Some, about ghosts and zombies, were no doubt apocryphal. I half snickered to myself. This whole insane thing had started in a cemetery, right? A ghostly presence in the New York Public Library could fit right in.

My uncle had told me other stories, like how he'd made out with a girl in the stacks. Who knew if that was true? What I did know is that there was something otherworldly, an aura of anything could happen, in those stacks. I'd really enjoyed my few visits, though by the time I'd first arrived there, the goblins were gone. And I wasn't able to prowl the stacks directly. The best I could do was ask a page – the great name for a library assistant who wasn't a librarian or even a clerk – to see if the stacks had a book I'd needed.

The stacks were now called the Milstein Research Stacks, and in 2016 a sophisticated conveyor system had been installed by Teledynamic, a company in New Jersey. I read all about that on a plaque on the wall in the lobby of the library. It advised people who needed books in the stacks to go to the Rose Reading Room or a room on the first floor. I went to the first-floor room – after all, I was on that floor right now.

There was another sign about the stacks right outside the room. They'd been expanded in new facilities under Bryant Park, right next to the library. I could make my request to a member of the "staff," who would put in my request to staff at the stacks. If the book or books I wanted were there, someone would put them on the conveyor back to this room.

I walked up to a woman who stood behind a counter. Judging by her age – which looked to be at least 75 or older – she was likely retired from whatever her life's work had been, and worked here as a volunteer. Lots of people who loved books did this.

She smiled at me and looked at my ID. "How can I assist you professor?"

"I'm researching androids – robots," I told her. "And I was wondering if you could get me the oldest book you have on the subject. Or books, if you have more than one." I'd thought this out on the train. I highly doubted there'd be a book with "Calculator" in the title – or, there were no doubt hundreds of books with the word in the title in the stacks, but they were about pocket calculators and all kinds of other calculators, not about Robinson or Lianne or John and their extended family.

The woman nodded and typed into her keyboard.

"Thank you, Ms. Lyncroft," I said, assuming she was the Davina

Lyncroft whose name was on a little Victorian nameplate on her counter. It looked old, but I assumed it was a repro.

"You're very welcome, professor," she said. "This could take a few minutes. You're welcome to wait in that chair," she pointed to a plush, oversized armchair. "We have very good wifi. You don't need a password."

"Thanks, I think I will," I smiled and went to the chair. It was even more comfortable than it looked.

I scrolled through my photos, on the chance that maybe I had accidentally repositioned the photo of the tombstone, perhaps inadvertently set it to a much earlier date. Or maybe I had somehow moved it to the "Recently deleted" folder. I found nada. I noted that every other single photo on my phone was exactly where I expected it to be. It was fun looking at them, though, hundreds of them—

"I'm sorry," Ms. Lyncroft interrupted my perusing about ten minutes later. "I just received a message from the stacks. Apparently the three oldest books with 'robot' or 'android' in the title have all gone missing."

"How could be that be?" I asked, surprised, trying not show I was also ... really annoyed. More than that. "Books from the stacks are not allowed in circulation, right?"

"Indeed," Lyncroft said and nodded. "We're looking into where the books are now. Likely they were mis-shelved. I'm sorry to say that sometimes happens."

"Mis-shelved by one of the staff?" I asked. "Or is it possible that someone got into the stacks from outside?"

"Oh no, I assure you," Lyncroft replied. "The only people allowed in those stacks are staff."

"I assume tracking those books down could take some time," I said.

"I'm afraid so, yes," Lyncroft said. "Could take days, even weeks. Those stacks are *huge*. If you give me your email, I can let you know as soon as I receive more information."

I gave her one of my cards. "Thank you," I said. "One more question. Could you give me the titles of those books? And their years of first publication?" I assumed the years were in the late 1920s, or after Čapek's *R.U.R.*

"Of course," Lyncroft said. "Give me a few minutes." She walked back to her desk.

She indeed returned a few minutes later with a piece a paper. The first thing I noticed was the year after each of the three titles. They were a hundred years earlier than what I'd expected.

***

I walked out of the library, into the sunlight, partially enlightened, partially in a stupor, born of bumping into something I could barely understand. Apparently the reach of the Calculators extended from erasing photos and words on tombstones to removing books from the New York Public Library stacks. Did someone by the name of Calculator work here?

I tried to focus on something that I'd just learned. Čapek had likely not invented the term 'robot,' but picked it up from usage a hundred years earlier. Likely Mary Shelley had picked up on that same undercurrent, if that's what it was, when she wrote *Frankenstein* a little before January, 1818, when the first edition was published. Ordinarily, that in itself would have been fascinating to know.

But it was just a footnote to what was flooding my head. The Calculators had powers that far exceeded hacking my phone or sandblasting their name off a tombstone in a public cemetery. They could get into the stacks of the New York Public Library – the soul of the Library, as I'd always thought of it – and remove the very books I was seeking. All within mere hours of my meeting John in the Indian Road Café, and less than an hour from when I'd decided to request those books from the stacks.

I cleared my throat and swallowed hard. What was my next move? Fly to another big city? New York of course wasn't the only city with a world-class library. I loved the library at the British Museum every bit as much as I loved the Library that loomed majestically behind me.

I sat on a step near a stone lion. The marble guardian had failed in its task, if any part of its job had been to protect the holdings of the library. And I had an unshakeable feeling that if I flew to every stately library cathedral in this world, the results would be the same as I'd just encountered here. The books I was seeking would be unaccountably missing.

I looked at the lion and nodded goodbye. Not your fault. There were things afoot, currents at large, that surpassed the power of any stone lion, or me, to stop or even slow down.

5

There was a message on my phone waiting for me when I ascended from the subway in Inwood. It was from Lianne. My heart jumped. I was relieved.

I walked to a nearby park bench and listened. "Don't try to return this call," she said. "I'm changing my number. But I wanted to tell you that I really enjoyed myself with you last night. And I wanted to apologize for erasing the photo on your phone and where you stored it online. I ... we're very skilled at that sort of thing. And look, I'm not saying we can never be together. It's just that ... the time is not right, not right now. Maybe sometime in the future." And she actually threw me a kiss. After all of this, a kiss.

***

I sulked the next few days. I taught my classes, moped around my office, and didn't do much of anything. Dave called me on the way home.

"My schedule finally cleared up. You free for a drink this afternoon?"

"Sure," I said, and suggested the Indian Road Café, because I didn't feel like traveling.

***

I met him there an hour later. I expected him not to show, or John Calculator to be there in his stead.

Dave ordered a beer. I ordered a Turkish wine. We looked at each other and both shook our heads.

"So, I gather you've been having a tough time of it," Dave said.

"I don't think you heard that from me," I replied, though I supposed I looked and sounded plenty beleaguered.

"No, not from you," Dave said. "They're much more powerful than you'd imagine. The digital revolution played right into their hands."

"Did they help create that?" I asked.

"Maybe, possibly, who knows? But they took to it like fish to water. The Calculators are, were, already digital in some sense."

Dave looked at the waiter who had arrived with our drinks. "Thank you," he said.

"Why did they put the name Robinson Calculator on that tombstone if they're so obsessed with secrecy?" I asked.

Dave took a long sip of his beer. "That's the question. Maybe to see what kind of reaction it would evoke?"

"Hmph," I said sarcastically. "Well, I guess I certainly provided them with more of an answer than they anticipated. Running around the city and Westchester, badgering everyone I could get into a conversation, to find out who the Calculators were." I almost added, and bedding Lianne, but I was able to contain myself.

"You don't know if you were the first one to see that tombstone, or how long it was there," Dave said.

I finally sipped some wine. It was good. The only comforting thing at this table. "You know, I don't recall seeing a date on the gravestone."

Dave nodded. "Well, that makes sense, I guess. If they were trying to see what kind of response that name on a tombstone would elicit, they would include as little specific information as possible. That would encourage anyone who saw it to wonder how it fit into their world. If there was a date of death before you even were born, that might make it seem less relevant to you."

"It was sheer luck that I even saw the damned thing," I said. "If I had just looked in any other direction at that moment, I wouldn't have seen it." Sheer luck? Sheer *bad* luck would be more like it. Maybe very bad luck, because it suddenly occurred to me that since I had indeed seen it, and had been making such a big deal about it, maybe the Calculators wanted to eliminate *me*. I'd admitted to Dave that I'd even intended to make a movie about the Calculators. Was he the hit man? My brain was racing. I wondered if maybe it had been planned for me to see that tombstone – but how could the Calculators have known that I'd be at the cemetery that day?

Dave looked at me a little oddly. "Don't beat yourself up about it."

I sipped and nodded. I had to resist being paranoid. Still, I had to be extremely careful now – in everything I did, in everything I said to Dave.   "Apropos your fish and water metaphor, I think I'm going to let all this be water under the bridge. Give my Calculator hunt a rest." I realized I was beginning to truly feel that if I never saw or heard the name Calculator again, that would be ok with me. Maybe I was just reacting to everything that had happened to me since that day at the cemetery, maybe my mind was just acting in its own best defense.

Dave nodded slowly. "I think that's a very good idea. Look, I was married and walked away. Your entanglement is almost entirely of your own making."

I drained my wine glass. I actually was beginning to feel a tiny bit better already. I had no idea how many Calculators there were in this world, but there couldn't be that many. I might never see another Calculator again unless I went looking for them. I looked around for our waiter to order another glass of wine.

Dave nursed his beer, smiled, and reached over to squeeze my shoulder. "It's not easy, I know. You're making the right decision."

I nodded. "I'm going to see if I can get more wine," I said. "Anything more for you?"

"I'm alright, thanks," Dave said.

I pushed my chair back, got up, and walked to the bar. Truthfully, I could still feel Lianne on top of me, I could still smell her hair, but I could get over her. I had to. I had to at least try. The movie wasn't all that important. Lianne somehow was. But I had to give forgetting her and the Calculators a shot. I had a feeling that maybe my life depended on it.

Our waiter, who had been talking to someone at the bar, turned around —"Apologies! Is there something else you wanted?"

"Yes." I told him I'd like another glass of the same wine.

"Of course!" he said. "I'll bring it right over to you."

"Thank you," I said, and started walking back to our table. It looked like Dave was talking to someone on the phone. He was nodding vigorously.

"—Oops, sorry!" I'd walked into someone, or he into me, and he was apologizing.

"It was me," I said. "I need to look where I am walking."

"No problem!" he said, and walked quickly to the door. He looked like a Kennedy, maybe JFK, if he'd lived to be 60.

I realized, after he'd left the Café, that our collision had caused him to drop something on the floor. It was right in front of me. It was a credit card.

I bent down and picked it up. The card was face down. I turned it over. The name read "Julian Calculator."

ABOUT THE AUTHOR

Paul Levinson, PhD, is Professor of Communication & Media Studies at Fordham University in NYC. His nonfiction books, including *The Soft Edge* (1997), *Digital McLuhan* (1999), *Realspace* (2003), *Cellphone* (2004), and *New New Media* (2009; 2nd edition, 2012), have been translated into fifteen languages. His science fiction novels include *The Silk Code* (winner of Locus Award for Best First Science Fiction Novel of 1999), *Borrowed Tides* (2001), *The Consciousness Plague* (2002), *The Pixel Eye* (2003), *The Plot To Save Socrates* (2006), *Unburning Alexandria* (2013), and *Chronica* (2014) — the last three of which are also known as the Sierra Waters trilogy, and are historical as well as science fiction. His novelette, "The Chronology Protection Case," was made into a short movie available on Amazon Prime. His alternate history story about The Beatles, "It's Real Life," was made into a radio play available on Audible. He appears on CNN, MSNBC, the Discovery Channel, National Geographic, the History Channel, NPR, and numerous TV and radio programs. His 1972 LP, *Twice Upon a Rhyme*, was re-issued in 2010; *Welcome Up: Songs of Space and Time*, his first new album since 1972, was released in 2020. He reviews television in his InfiniteRegress.tv blog.

The following books by Paul Levinson are available in paperback and on Kindle:

Nonfiction:

The Soft Edge: A Natural History and Future of the Information Revolution

Digital McLuhan: A Guide to the Information Millennium

McLuhan in an Age of Social Media

Realspace: The Fate of Physical Presence in the Digital Age, On and Off Planet

New New Media

From Media Theory to Space Odyssey: Petar Jandrić interviews Paul Levinson

Cyber War and Peace

Human Replay: A Theory of the Evolution of Media, original PhD dissertation, New York University, 1979

Fake News in Real Context

Science fiction:

Loose Ends (time travel) series (complete):
Loose Ends, Little Differences, Late Lessons, Last Calls

Sierra Waters (time travel) series:
The Plot to Save Socrates, Unburning Alexandria, Chronica

Phil D'Amato forensic detective series:
The Chronology Protection Case, The Silk Code, The Consciousness Plague, The Pixel Eye

Ian's Ions and Eons (three time travel novelettes)

Exo-Genetic Engineers series:
The Orchard, The Suspended Fourth

Borrowed Tides

Double Realities series: It's Real Life, The Other Car, Extra Credit, The Wallet, The P&A

The Kid in the Video Store

Marilyn and Monet

Robinson Calculator

Peter Brown Called: Tales of SciFi and Music

Nonfiction and Science Fiction

Touching the Face of the Cosmos: On the Intersection of Space Travel and Religion
an anthology of essays and science fiction stories, including a new interview with John Glenn, an essay by Guy Consolmagno, SJ (the "Pope's Astronomer"), and contributions from leading thinkers about the role of religion in space travel

THE
SILK CODE

PAUL
LEVINSON

"An impressive debut"-Joe Haldeman

"Delivers on its promises"-The New York Times Book Review

THE PLOT TO SAVE

SOCRATES

PAUL LEVINSON

"A tour de force" — *Analog*
"challenging fun" —*Entertainment Weekly*